Shadow Animals

a Meridian Codex story

KEITH DEININGER

First Edition

www.KeithDeininger.com

Cover design by Sumrow Art and Illustration

New Release Mailing List
Join Keith's mailing list to receive a free story, the occasional bonus material, and be the first to hear when he has a new release. (keithdeininger.com/new-release-mailing-list)

Twitter: twitter.com/keithdeininger
Facebook: facebook.com/keith.deininger
Goodreads: goodreads.com/keithdeininger

ALSO BY KEITH DEININGER

<u>NOVELS</u>

The New Flesh

Ghosts of Eden (Nov. 2014)

Within (May 2015)

<u>NOVELLAS</u>

Fevered Hills

Marrow's Pit

The Hallow (Feb. 2015)

For my parents, who allowed me to be different, and, oh, the results…

ACKNOWLEDGEMENTS

Special thanks to those who have supported my work and given me the confidence to continue this insane pursuit of writing fiction; to John Sumrow, who designed the cover and encouraged me to pursue all avenues of publishing; to my wife Amber, of course, who knows how important my writing is to me; and especially to Shelley Milligan and Kimberly Yerina who have been advocates of my work from the very beginning and, having read the early versions, have always known exactly what is needed—I can't thank you enough!

Also, a special thanks to those reviewers who spread the word and keep the conversation alive. Reading is intellectual freedom!

"It seems to me I am trying to tell you a dream—making a vain attempt, because no relation of a dream can convey the dream-sensation, that commingling of absurdity, surprise, and bewilderment in a tremor of struggling revolt, that notion of being captured by the incredible which is of the very essence of dreams...No, it is impossible; it is impossible to convey the life-sensation of any given epoch of one's existence—that which makes its truth, its meaning—its subtle and penetrating essence. It is impossible. We live, as we dream—alone..."
— Joseph Conrad, *Heart of Darkness*

There was a map my son had found somewhere on the wall of my study back home and sometimes, coming back late from a long weekend trip up river, I'd lie on the couch and look at it, too tired to do anything else. That map was amazing, especially because it wasn't of any place real. It was very old, the only one like it I'd ever seen. Its edges were curled and frayed by the dry heat of the desert, revealing a deep orange parchment beneath, the land it depicted appearing dull and ancient, snaking roads and the Purgatoire River going on and on. "That's old," I'd tell my wife whenever she came in to check on me, it's probably not like that anymore.

My son used to play alone along the banks of the arroyo where we live in the southwestern United States— in Copperton, New Mexico, named for the color of the leaves during the fall season—where the waters trickle sluggishly in gray rivulets through the sand, trees yellowish and drooping. Once a year, the rains come and don't let up for days, hammering the roof of our house, rattling the windows, smearing the dust down the glass in messy slug trails. The arroyo fills with water, sometimes suddenly, a hollow roar you can hear miles off, echoing through the valley from one mountain top to the next like titanic conspirators. For several days, the storms rage. People carry umbrellas and wear black rubber boots as they dash to their cars, driving slowly through several inches of runoff, white cascades of slush flying through the air as they thump through the deeper puddles, on their way to work, or the grocery store for batteries and canned food in case the electricity goes out again. Then, just as suddenly as it begins, the rain sputters out and dies. The water level in the arroyo immediately descends, flows away downstream and is gone, becomes nothing but a dull dribble.

My son, overly excited at finally being able to go outside, rushing down to the creek to see what the waters have brought this time. The sun comes out and, for a little while, the air is hung with a vaporous veil of moisture. My son collects things, shows me his discoveries with the gleaming eyes of a mad professor, licking his lips over and over again as he waves his hands over his treasure trove: river-smoothed stones of colored marble, pale pink, turquoise and amber; driftwood shaped like animals, like small rodents, a log like an alligator; a crushed and twisted ball of wire like a man-made tumbleweed; a mattress like a small raft, sticks and branches piercing it like spears, splattered with dark stains; a skull from an animal of some sort, a fox or badger; a couple of ribs, pieces of fractured spine; an entire refrigerator, missing everything inside except for a few brown condiment bottles in the door rack; a child's plastic doll with a man's belt pulled tightly about its neck; and next to that a small collection of children's tennis shoes; and next to that an assortment of vessels, plastic tubs, and canning jars, and a porcelain dog bowl with the name "Ralph" carved into it; and next to that a small statuette, perhaps broken from the top of a trophy, of a woman holding something, but whatever it is—a broom? a golf club? a rifle? a ceremonial knife?—is missing and likely lost forever.

And then there are the stranger items, many of which I have saved and now lurk on the shelf in my study: a dark, wooden flute; a curve-bladed karambit; the corroded remains of a pistol made from iron, branded in an unknown language; a small metal chair figurine on a chain to be worn around the neck; a wicker box filled with shriveled ears, purplish in color; a plaque carved with a complex, geometrical design from another world; a tangle of lace that might have been a wedding veil; a scimitar; something like a wine bladder made from an unknown animal, still fragrant from the acrid liquid that once filled it; a jar of rare and unusual pickled insects, and another jar of eyes, perfectly preserved, of such variety, occupying a central place of honor on the shelf in my study: some round and yellow, some almond-shaped, others with striations of veins, and still others with misshapen pupils, some purely black; blues, and browns, and reds; some nictitating and others with tapetum lucidum; from animals and people of such diversity many of them could only have come from the region upriver, where my son has gone, where he has become lost—stolen from me, and my wife— where I now camp amongst the dark trees, travelling alone, praying I'll be the first to find him, the shadows chasing us both.

Saul looked up into the tree; he'd been here before, although he couldn't remember ever having come this far up the river. It was larger than any tree he'd ever seen, it's girth rolling upwards, branches reaching out and up to regions he thought, if he'd been able to draw a sightline through the dense canopy of dipping leaves like baby blankets in the dark, must be further than the eye could see, where the air was thin. Its roots twisted into the earth, giant organic sheets, creating crevasses of safety, one of which had become his campsite for the night. His fire glowed dully within his crevasse like a cave. It was strange: he'd forgotten all about this tree. He'd climbed in it once, when he was a child, but his memories were vague and he was old now; he felt old. His fish sputtered in its own grease in the skillet he'd lain over the coals. He was moving as quickly as he could, as many miles as he could each day, but he had to keep up his strength; he had to hunt and fish, since there was only so much he could carry, and he was on foot, which slowed his progress. Fortunately, the river was teeming with fish, from trout and bass to those he couldn't name—black and white striped, or with tufts of mousey hair—and it didn't take long to catch his supper. There was also plenty of game, but he wasn't much good with the rifle or with traps and such tasks would require more effort and hours in the day than he was willing to expend.

Only yesterday he'd found their campsite. They'd tried to conceal it, brushing away their tracks, scattering the stones from their fire and covering the ashes with boughs they'd trimmed from the bushes nearby, but he'd seen their marks. He'd seen the ashes staining the soil dark and, darker still, signs of their religious practices, mists pooling in the depressions left by their digging, tiny dolls made from husks of vegetation, discarded in the dust.

He was catching up.

He knew he was getting closer because Ezzy, short for Ezekiel, had left him clues. He'd found scraps of clothing tied conspicuously to bushes, flapping in the wind. He'd found marks in the sand—not words; nothing his son would be caught by his captors doing—but a small "X" or "O" from time to time. Once, he'd found a pile of leaves ripped into shapes resembling animals, like the ones his son was so good at making in the shadows on the wall using his hands against a lamp late at night.

Saul, wrapped in his sleeping bag, lay in the crook of the tree, and closed his eyes. He didn't have a tent, but he did have a tarp—a cheap plastic thing he'd purchased at Wal-Mart before embarking on this journey, that was already tearing—tied over his head. The night air was cooling quickly, but there was no threat of rain. Against the tree he felt safe.

He knew only a little of what stalked him. His father had spoken of it once, but he'd never seen it. He knew only that it was something looming, a powerful presence few had dared challenge. He didn't know why it came after him now. Did it need a reason? It was unnamable; no one had ever had the courage to give it a designation. It didn't move fast, was all he knew. He had to keep moving. If he kept moving, he might be okay.

At daybreak he'd be on his weary feet again, and he'd be pushing himself to move as quickly as he could. If there was any other way for him to travel he would have found it. He certainly couldn't drive his old, beat-up Toyota truck up here, the ground was too rocky, the trees too dense, even too much for a motorcycle or dirt bike. On horseback, maybe? But there were places, where the vines hung down from above and the brush beneath tangled in clumps, which would be difficult even for a horse to traverse, even if he had managed to acquire one. He had neighbors in Copperton who kept horses, of course, but he'd never been close with his neighbors.

Finally, he drifted into sleep and dreamed his son was standing on a small rise at the other side of a great grove of trees filled with mist that made it impossible to cross. He called out to his son, but even though Ezzy's face was obscured in shadow, he could tell his son was crying, shaking with fear. His son lifted his hand out, as if he might grasp Saul—his beloved father, his protector— through all that distance. The trees shook and the collective roaring noise of thousands of animals filled the air, and eyes of many various shapes and sizes opened and glowed from the shadows.

* * *

In the morning, he packed quickly. He kicked dirt over his fire, rolled up his tarp and sleeping bag, tightened the laces on his hiking boots, and was on his way. He ate a few mixed nuts from what was now a small baggy that he'd brought with him, as he kicked his legs forward, forcing circulation into them. His bottle was filled with water he'd boiled over the fire the night before from which he periodically drank. He forged his path, always going upriver, deeper into the unknown, always upriver.

By mid-morning he was struggling. The ground had begun to soften and there were patches of reed-lined mud buzzing with biting flies that threatened to suck the boots right off his feet. He was forced to move slowly, being as careful as he could be. He lost the trail; there were no more visible signs left by his son. He was forced to go around certain swampy patches, straying further and further from the river, and he was afraid, at times, of becoming lost. The river was his guide; as long as he followed the river, he knew he was going in the right general direction.

Somewhere in the forest, it was impossible to tell how close or how far away as it echoed through the trees, a bird made a sound like laughter. The sun had gone behind some clouds and it was now gray and damp in the forest. He was sweating, his clothes hanging soggy over his shoulders. The ferns were replaced with trembling clots of moss like spider's sacks.

He trampled the foliage with his boots, no longer possessing the energy to pick his steps carefully. When his foot dropped into another mud bog, he tore it free and moved forward blindly. His cheek bled where a branch had whipped it. He was panting, out of breath. Only the day before, he'd moved easily, the ground soft and spongy with fallen needles from the pines. Now, each step was an effort and he'd lost the trail to his son.

He stopped to catch his breath, the dry lining of his throat feeling as if it absorbed the water he poured down it before it even hit his stomach. He felt sick, despair and hopelessness sinking into him as a stone sinks in a scummy pond. Before him was the largest patch of swamp he'd seen so far. He knew he'd have to turn west and travel even further from the river to go around it. He could feel whatever hunted him getting closer. Whatever it was, it didn't move like he did, it wasn't slowed by difficult terrain. In his mind he heard the laughing bird again. He grimaced and forced himself to move.

He'd never been this far upriver before. He couldn't remember ever encountering a swampy region. But, then again, maybe he had. It had been many years since he'd come this far, and the forest had a way of changing on you, often in surprising and unusual ways.

Only earlier that morning, as he'd passed between the trees, he'd heard a noise, stopped, and seen an elk so large he'd had to rub his eyes to be sure he was actually seeing it. Mostly what he saw were its muscular legs, thick as tree trunks, and the mass of its body, its flat-ridged antlers rising above the canopy of the trees. There had still been mist in the air and when the animal moved Saul had felt the ground tremble. He'd thought briefly of trying to slay the elk with his rifle for his supper, but quickly given up the idea as he knew the animal was too large to kill with his rifle alone, and then it was gone.

"Hey, mister? You lost or something?"

Saul jumped, ripped from his thoughts, his hands grappling awkwardly for his rifle. He swung around, glancing through the trees.

"Right here," the voice said.

He glanced up and realized there was someone crouched on a branch in one of the trees almost directly in front of him. He lifted the rifle; its barrel shook visibly.

"You make an awful lot of noise, you know that?" And, to Saul's complete surprise, the owner of that voice smiled at him, an easy smile—the kind of smile one might give an old friend over a tumbler of brandy by a fire indoors.

16

The figure dropped easily from the tree, landing on a clear and solid patch of soil and stood before him. She was a woman—well, a girl; she was young, a teenager perhaps. She had straight, dark hair that bobbed casually just above her shoulders and a smooth, small-featured face.

"I've been following you for a while now, but you seem to be having a tough time," she said. "Maybe I can help."

Saul let the rifle drop to his side. "Do you know how to get out of this damn swamp?"

The girl smiled. "Oh yeah. Of course. No problem. Follow me."

"Wait," Saul said. The girl stopped. "Who are you?"

"I'm Koryn."

"Where did you come from?"

"I'm not supposed to come out here so don't tell anyone. Are you trying to reach the Great Wall? You're closer than you think." She darted into the bushes.

"Wait!"

Koryn looked back.

"Have you seen anyone?"

Koryn scowled. "Why?"

Saul staggered up to the girl. "They have my boy. Have you seen a young boy with blonde hair?"

Koryn dropped her eyes. "Is *that* who you're after?"

Saul looked closely into Koryn's face. "Yes. Have you seen my boy?"

"Yeah, I saw him, but I wouldn't mess with the shadow animals."

Saul gripped his rifle across his chest. "I know. But I have to. They have my son. Do you know where they're going?"

"Sure."

"Will you show me?"
"Yeah, okay."

* * *

He followed Koryn. The path she forged was winding and, at least as it appeared to Saul, a series of random turns left and then right and then right again and then left, yet she led him successfully out of the bog and the ground became firm again and easily travelled. He could no longer hear the comforting flow of the river, but he trusted Koryn, she seemed to know what she was doing and in which direction she was going.

"I'm from Sage," she told him, when the path widened enough for the two of them to walk side by side. "It's a small village not far from here. It's boring."

Saul scowled to himself, trying to remember. "Have you lived there long?"

Koryn skipped up and over a jutting tree trunk. "My whole life. I've always played in these woods."

"Isn't that dangerous? What do your parents think of that?"

"Oh, they don't know how far I go. They think I stay close to town. They think I'm staying at my friend Jenna's house tonight, in fact."

Saul could vaguely remember visiting some place with his father; he could remember his father talking about a tiny village upriver.

"My mom is always talking about these woods," Koryn said. "She says that every forest has a dark heart at its center. She says the dark heart breeds dark things. I saw a lizard once with a forked tongue and three tails. I tried to catch it, but it was too fast. I guess that's what she means.

Mutant things. You just have to know which places to stay out of."

Saul shrugged. "Yeah. I guess so."

"We're not gonna make it there by nightfall," Koryn said.

"We're not?"

Koryn shook her head. "Nope. The Great Wall is too far from here. We should find a place to camp."

"The Great Wall? Is that where they've taken my son?"

"Where else would they go? Besides, I know someone there who can help."

Saul didn't reply. What choice did he have? He'd long ago lost the trail—his tracking skills being rather limited—and he knew his best chance was with this girl as his guide.

"Koryn?" he asked.

She turned to look at him, her eyes bright. "Yeah?"

"How old are you?"

She smiled. "Fifteen." She darted through the trees.

* * *

That evening, by the glow of the fire, glimmering high on her cheeks and impish nose, Koryn said, "I sleep in the trees mostly, when I camp out. I feel safe in the trees. But I'll sleep on the ground with you tonight. I feel safe with you."

Saul rubbed his hands together, then held his palms out to the fire. "This is your forest. You know it better than I do."

Koryn smiled slightly, her lips twitching, flickering. "Yes. But you're the one with the gun."

Saul didn't reply. They were silent for a time. The fire spat and sparked as it consumed a knot of wood.

Quietly, tentatively, "What's your son's name?"

"Ezekiel, but we call him Ezzy. He's nine years old."

Koryn's eyes were hidden in shadow. "That's really sad he's lost. Did he run away?"

Saul sighed heavily. "He likes to play in the forest, like you. One day, he didn't come back for dinner. My wife and I always knew there were dangerous things in the woods, but we also knew they never came far downriver. We never thought our son would wander far enough to—" He couldn't speak.

Koryn said, "Oh," then was silent.

The flames danced like spirits seeking the freedom of the night.

After a few minutes, Saul reached his hand down into his pack, all the way to the bottom, feeling around for something. He swallowed dryly. He removed the object: a book, plain and brown, like an encyclopedia, turning it in the firelight so that its gold-gilded title glistened as if wet. It was *Unusual Landscapes: Amazing Places of the World*. Written by a man by the name of William M. Gately and published in 1974, *Unusual Landscapes* contained the only description, however brief, of the Copperton Forest and the Purgatoire River Saul had ever found. According to the librarians he'd corresponded with, it had never been reprinted beyond its initial thousand copy first edition, one copy of which he'd managed to purchase for a substantial sum on eBay, and he'd never seen another for sale since.

"You mind if I read you something?"

Koryn shook her head. "Go ahead."

Saul opened the book to the section he had marked with a folded corner. He cleared his throat and turned the open pages to the firelight. "It was Francisco Vasquez de Coronado himself who first reported seeing unusually large beasts in the Copperton Forest of what is now southern New Mexico. According to his journals, he claims to have come upon a winding river that grew ever wider and 'most furious' as he and his companions travelled up it. He claims to have seen a saber-toothed tiger and a small predatory cat with spots like a cheetah, and he claims one of his men to have seen a wooly mammoth in the mists crashing through the trees one morning. These animals are, of course, known to be long ago extinct, but there is evidence that some of these animals may still survive on the upper reaches of Purgatoire Creek, whose waters dry by the time they reach the town of Copperton itself. To this day, hunters in the Copperton Forest sometimes report sighting massive beasts with dark and matted hair like a human's and reptilian creatures the size of dogs with aubergine spots. Perhaps these tales are nothing more than the embellishments of weary hunters living in such a remote and unpopulated region, or perhaps…" Saul stopped, taking a drink from his canteen. He cleared his throat. "And it goes on from there," he said. He watched Koryn for her reaction.

Koryn returned his gaze. "So?"

"This book is about some really strange places in the world and it includes the Copperton Forest. Why? It describes the Chocolate Hills in the Philippines, the Moeraki Boulders in New Zealand that were formed sixty-five million years ago and look like massive cracked eggs, the Darvaza Gas Crater in Turkmenistan that excavators lit in 1971 and that still burns to this day, the Naigu Stone

Forest in China, and the four islands of the Socotra Archipelago where some of the weirdest plants in the world grow like the dragon's blood tree and the desert rose. But why do you think it also includes the Copperton Forest? I've read this book extensively, as you can tell. What do you think, Koryn—who has lived her entire life here? Have you ever seen a wooly mammoth or saber-toothed tiger in these woods?"

Koryn stared at him, her mouth open slightly, her eyes reflecting orange the firelight. "I...I don't think so. What's a wooly mammoth?"

"They're huge and hairy and... Never mind. It doesn't matter. It's just, I've given up being shocked by some of the weird things I see in these woods. I just...I want my son back. I'm worried about him."

"I know," Koryn said. "I'm sorry."

"I hope you can help me."

Koryn looked serious. "I can."

"Good. That's good. Because I have no idea what I'm doing."

Koryn smiled. "It's okay. I know what took him. Galen will know where he is."

"Galen?"

"He lives on the other side of the Great Wall. I'll show you."

Saul watched Koryn closely. She didn't seem to be lying, too innocent to be telling untruths. He nodded assent. "You mind if I write in my journal now? I've been writing in it every night, trying to keep my memories straight this time."

"Sure. I'll be quiet." Koryn poked the fire idly with a stick.

She watched Saul bring out his notebook and pen, watched him look over what he'd written the night before, but wasn't bothered by her curiosity. Before he began, he looked at *Unusual Landscapes* one last time, still open in his lap. He read the final paragraph of the page-and-a-half section on the Copperton Forest, as he had hundreds of times before:

The mysterious qualities of the Copperton Forest to exceed the factual elements of the rationally explained, and to maintain its elusive nature of relative indefinability, may, in fact, be an extension of man's inability to civilize that which it fails to understand. This fantastic region—its indigenous life far exceeding in quantity and variety any other single region on Earth—remains unmapped by any official means. Indeed, the Purgatiore River itself is marked only as a tributary through southwestern Colorado winding northeastward for only about 200 miles, never going further south than the Arkansas river, where it "officially" drains, certainly never reaching the southern region of the state of New Mexico. There are no recorded texts of the exotic wildlife known to exist along the Purgatiore River in the deeper regions of the Copperton Forest beyond the personal journals of certain explorers, such as Francisco Coronado, nor of the people who dwell beyond the "impenetrable face of the green mountain," with their strange and shamanistic ways. The United States

Geographical Survey has released only this official statement regarding the Copperton Forest region: "Despite receiving several reports concerning the region, the USGS is unable to verify the location of the Copperton Forest or the stretch of the Purgatoire River said to flow through it and must therefore conclude its existence to be nothing more than rumor and hearsay, much like the famed gold-laden city of El Dorado."

* * *

Later—the fire burned down to coals like fiery, warming gems—Saul lay with his head resting on his backpack and closed his eyes. He was drifting when Koryn came to lie beside him. He could already tell it was going to be a cold night and Koryn had only her cloak and he his sleeping bag. She snuggled against him, turned away, the shape of her body against his; her hair smelled sweet like the forest. He couldn't help but be stirred by her curves, young and smooth, yet womanly. "You can if you want," Koryn whispered, feeling his stiffening warmth. "I don't mind." He put his hand on the up-rise of her hip.

Saul shifted away, pulling his hand back, laying the other way. He thought of Helen, his wife, waiting for him back home, her hair long, the color of morning beach sand, even as it'd been when he'd left her, greasy and unkempt.

* * *

He awoke abruptly to Koryn sitting up with a jerk. Through sleep-slackened eyes, he blinked up at Koryn's darkened face staring down at him in complete terror. She raised her hands, making claws of them, as if to attack him, then turned them on herself, raking her cheeks, then dropped her face into her palms and sobbed.

Saul sat up and took the girl in his arms. "Koryn? What's wrong? It was just a dream, just a bad dream. Shhh. It's okay."

She screamed into her hands. "I saw it! What is it? What's chasing you?"

Saul's heart jumped in his chest.

Ezzy had only been missing for two days when my wife gave up hope. It happened abruptly. She simply stopped eating and her eyes grew distant and glazed. She knew where our son had gone; she knew he was lost. Those who went too deeply into the Copperton Forest never came back, and if they did return, were never the same thereafter. The authorities promised to help with the search, after the allotted legal time period, but even they knew they'd never find our son, not, at least, where they were looking.

I remember how she looked when I told her I was going after our son. I told her what I'd found: a spot along the river where there was evidence of a struggle and Ezzy's baseball cap lying in the sand. I told her how I'd heard there were strange things about in the Copperton Forest, things that didn't belong. I told her our son had been taken.

"Don't you see, Helen?" I said. "I have to go after him. I have to rescue him. There's no one else."

Helen nodded vaguely from amongst the yellowing sheets on the bed.

"I have to try. I can't just sit here and do nothing. Okay?"

Helen stared at her curled and motionless hands in her lap.

"I'm going to the store for supplies. Then I'm heading out. You'll have to take care of yourself for a couple of days. Okay?"

*Helen looked up at me then, and for a brief moment,
she was my wife again, meeting my gaze with intense
emotion-filled eyes—then she dropped her head, and
slumped against the wall.*

It was enough. That look was all the assent I needed.

*I left her like that. There was little else I could do
for her anyway. There's everything she needs in the house;
I made sure of that. She'll be okay.*

This forest. This damn forest.

*Even as a kid I'd always known there was something
unusual about the territory upriver from our house, and
my father knew the same thing, and likely his father before
him. When I was little, I used to hike up to where the creek
became a stream and the waters made a soothing bubbling
noise as they tumbled through the rocks, and you could
find deeper pools beneath shaded boulders where fish
could be caught that shone luminesce in the sun.
Sometimes, my father would take me a little further—on
weekend camping trips—where the waters began to widen
and splash white against the rocks, where he taught me
how to hunt, how to fire a rifle, although I was never very
good, nor had I the stomach for it. He used to snatch the
rifle from my trembling hands because he'd lost patience
with me, set it effortlessly in the crook of his shoulder, and
slay the ibex eating leaves in a copse of trees in front of us
with a single shot. Sometimes, when we reached the body
of the ibex, with its intricate horns that curved outwards
and backwards, and I saw the blood, I couldn't hold back
the tears and my father would call me a sissy. Sometimes
he hit me with the back of his hand, or used his belt when
we got back to camp.*

*Other times, my father would wrap his brawny arm
around my skinny shoulders as we huddled by the fire at*

night with his chin turned out, eyes on the stars above. He could point out and name most of the major constellations. "Although it's difficult to make out," he'd say. "There's Virgo. See. Those faint stars form the head and body around the single bright star of Spica. And that circle there with the long tail is Pisces, the fish. And over there is Canis Major, the Great Dog." Times like that I'd look at my father and I'd ask him how he knew such things. "Knowledge is important, Saul," he'd say. "I spend a great deal of time reading and you should too. Do you know of Plato, or Descartes, or Marrow, or Confucius?" I'd shake my head. "You will learn. When you are older, I will teach you."

I think I was nine years old when my father died. He'd lost his job at the plant and had been supporting me and my mom with various temporary work, but it wasn't enough. To ease the burden, he'd take his rifle and go on hunting trips upriver into the Copperton Forest. At first, they were only short trips. He'd leave the house at just after noon and return that same evening with a strap of fish slung over his shoulder or a couple of squirrels or rabbits. But then the trips became longer. Sometimes he'd stay out overnight, or a couple of nights. He told my mom the game were getting scarce, wise to his recent hunting activities, and he had to hike up further and further. He starting bringing back larger game: deer and ibex; once he brought home a fox; another time a pair of long-bodied river otters. My mom didn't like to cook the stranger animals, but my dad skinned them and butchered them in the shed and brought my mom the meat in neat slices, almost as good as the pink steaks or ham hocks wrapped in cellophane from the grocery store. Personally, I didn't mind the meat, tasted just fine to me. Then, one day, my father never came back. He went too far; someone must have caught him; something must have happened. That was the only time I ever saw my mother cry. I think she cried because she knew how hard it was going to be for us with my dad gone, more so than because he was dead.

After that, I stopped going upriver much. I just sort of forgot about it. The memory of those waters never disappearing completely, but fading, becoming dull, like the memory of my father. If you went far enough, I knew, there was a small village. My father had taken me there only once before his death. It was a place I never forgot, although, for many years, I didn't believe it was real.

It was very dark in the forest. It grew darker and darker the deeper they travelled. Saul hiked steadily and Koryn led the way, surefooted and confident. The temperature dropped, but the exertion of their movements kept them warm. Koryn had her cloak tied about her throat so that it billowed around her, keeping in her body heat. Saul was wearing an old sweater.

They walked in amiable silence; it no longer seemed appropriate for them to speak. The forest had folded over them, felt as if its presence loomed above, more than just the trees now, more than the oily wood and spongy ground. Everywhere there was wildlife, the croaking sounds of birds and insects, reptilian things clutching low-hanging branches, scuttling in the underbrush, and the stench of moist carrion soil turned by worms.

When Koryn came to a halt, Saul felt as if he was in a trance, nearly bumping into her. He stopped himself, shook his head to clear it, and looked around. Koryn didn't say anything, but she was looking up. It was very dark in this region, and Saul quickly saw the reason for such darkness.

In front of them, rising higher than his eyes could see, was a massive and very-steep mountain. It was composed mostly of crumbling boulders, crawling with moss, stacked as if by crude, arcane giants. In some places, various forms of vegetation struggled from between cracks in the rock. It seemed impregnable, stretching distantly to their right and to their left, and there was some other quality about the mountain—it was forbidding; it made Saul wish he'd never seen it, that he should turn his back on it now, and return home.

Koryn said something.

"I'm sorry?"

"Here it is," Koryn said, not much louder than before.

"Here's what?"

"The Great Wall."

Saul looked up again. "Wall? This is no wall. This is a mountain."

"Nope. This is the Great Wall. Kinda freaky, huh?"

Saul looked closely at the boulders—yes, he could see they were all of relatively the same size. And yes, they appeared to be stacked, except for those that had crumbled and fallen loose. What had Gately called it in *Unusual Landscapes*? The "impenetrable face of the green mountain." A shiver ran through him.

"It marks the border," Koryn said. "But I know a way in."

Saul followed Koryn quickly as she began to take the path of crushed leaves along the side of the wall. They were forced to divert around several of the fallen boulders, one of them that, upon turning his head to glance back, appeared to Saul to have a smiling face carved into it.

"I knew we were close," Koryn said, stopping suddenly. "See." She pointed to a patch of foliage, a thick weave of hanging vines groping from one of the boulders.

Saul shook his head. "What?"

Koryn approached the wall of vines and began to pull on them, one at a time. "I know it's one of these." She pulled a vine, hissed, and drew her hand back. "Ouch," she said. "Thorns," sucking childishly on her bleeding finger.

"They don't know it's here," she said as she moved on to the next set of vines.

"Who doesn't?"

Koryn didn't reply. She seemed to find the vine she was looking for and pulled. The foliage rustled; there was a groaning sound.

"Come on," Koryn said, using her hands to part the foliage like a beard.

Saul swallowed dryly, and pushed through.

* * *

"Just follow me and don't talk to anyone and don't stop," Koryn said.

Saul followed closely behind his guide. They were in a dark tunnel, festooned with dripping vines.

Then, quite abruptly, they came out onto a narrow and abandoned cobblestone street. Koryn moved quickly and Saul didn't have much time to take in his surroundings, only the height of the buildings looming over them.

"This Galen guy, are you sure he can help?"

Koryn looked over her shoulder. "And whatever you do, don't stare," she said and disappeared through a cramped archway.

Saul stepped into the murk. Instantly, it was dark. Shadows caroused about him like a living substance. The air was colder, musty; the odor of mold seeped from the walls. Koryn was only visible as an apparition sliding forward in front of him. He scrambled after her, coming out into a small courtyard.

"This is Luto's Court," Koryn said, glancing about. "I know how to get to Galen's place. He'll be able to help. But beyond that—" She shrugged. "I'd probably get lost."

"What's that?" Saul asked, indicating a crumbling stone statue at the center of the small courtyard.

"That's Luto. Look if you want, but then we'd better go. We don't want to stay in one place for too long around here. We don't want to be noticed."

Saul stepped up to the statue. It was of a tall man standing in the dramatic pose of a war hero, humbled of detail through the years by the weather and lack of care, now indistinct stone. About its base, there was a plaque on which raised lettering had been rubbed to near illegibility, like those on an ancient headstone:

Luto Alexandero
The Great Architect
"All man needs is shelter."
"Welcome to the city of freedom!"

Saul turned to see Koryn shaking her head in disgust. "He built this place?" he asked her.

"Designed it. Slaves built it. Come on. We better go." She pointed to a dark opening like a subterranean tunnel across the courtyard Saul had failed to notice.

Koryn whisked forward. Saul followed, this passageway narrower than the last. He stepped in something soggy that seemed to move under his foot and he stumbled. He hurried on.

To Saul, the space around him seemed vaguely like a prison, or like the slums he'd seen in movies; it was like a drawing M. C. Escher might scribble in a nightmare. The entire compound seemed made from blocks lifted and

33

suspended on strings, dangling over their heads and connected by crisscrossing bridges so numerous they blocked out the sun.

They came out into a small alleyway clearing, several passages branching from it in various directions. Three ragged men stood from where they'd been crouching against the wall by a single light from one of the tunnels and shambled toward them. Koryn turned to them and flashed something from inside her cloak. The men stopped and whispered amongst themselves. The men slunk back into the shadows and slumped against the wall, sinking into their coats that seemed to writhe about them like living membranes.

"We have to hurry," Koryn said.

"Why?"

"Because they know we're here."

Saul felt his heart lurch in his chest.

In a dream I watched:

"No, Ja, I want it now."

"You'll just be hungry again in a moment, I'm afraid, Ji. Hold still. We're waiting for our call."

"But look at it, Ja. So pretty. A pretty kitty. Come here pretty kitty—" A hand reaches out, large and pale, with smooth, many-jointed fingers like emaciated arthritic snakes. The tiny furred animal trapped in the corner of the room shakes with terror, liquid silver eyes darting and rolling.

Ja pulls the hand back. "You fool. That's no kitty. That's a kylix."

Ji's round, unblinking eyes widen. "Ooo, a kylix."

The phone fills the tiny room with its blaring. Ja picks the red plastic receiver from its wall mount with his smaller, more human-looking hand, and places it near his face. "Yes?"

After a moment listening he says, "Excellent. We'll be right there." He replaces the phone on its hook. Tendrils of shadow shift like living nightmares from beneath his immaculate bowler hat. "They're going exactly where we thought they'd go. They're meeting Galen in Luto's Court."

"Here kitty, kitty," Ji says, stretching toward the Kylix. "Here pretty kitty. Come here."

"We'll come up right beneath them." Ja pushes some buttons on the control panel, then taps the 'up' key.

There is a ping sound, and the screech of old wires and gears; the elevator begins reluctantly to crawl upward.

Ji's hand reaches for the kylix.

"It's a pity these animals think they're safe to nest down here," Ja says.

The kylix makes a desperate leap, but Ji's hand is almost supernaturally fast, snatching the animal from the air. The kylix swings its tail, impaling Ji's arm with needle-sharp spines. Ji's large slobbering mouth grins, unmindful of the animal's attacks on his arm. There is snapping, and wet plopping sounds. Ji lifts the furry corpse toward his hole of teeth already gnashing in anticipation.

"As always, if you must." Ja turns his attention away.

The gears squeal and crunch as the elevator grinds steadily upward.

Luto's Court was unlike anywhere Saul had ever been. Crooked streets wound in every direction, disappearing into alleyways ending in dark, seedy taverns or unwelcoming shops with simple names like *Apothecary*, or *Drexel's*, or *The Bottling Yard*. Through the labyrinthine passages, Saul saw a tired warren of cramped streets and buildings that leaned like misaligned teeth, tiny frosted portal windows and narrow doors, obscured faces that peeked mistrustfully over balconies. Crumbled carts of moldering hay lay amongst battered tin trash cans and discarded detritus smashed beyond recognition. Clothing drooped over lines strung between buildings like shuddering phantoms. Wet trash lay kicked and trampled about their feet. Neon signs glowed feebly in the gloom: *Live Show* and *Chester's Place* and *Girls-Girls-Girls*.

Ahead of them, a woman leaned over an unstable railing and overturned a bucket. Slimy drippings seemed to evaporate before they struck the street. A man with his face shadowed under what looked to Saul like a sombrero passed by riding a forlorn beast with long tangled hair that grew down over its body and dragged behind it through the streets like a dirty dish rag. A woman with straight black hair tugged a child by a rope down one of the dark passageways and then they were gone.

"You have to be careful," Koryn said. "Most of the street signs are missing." She stopped for a moment. "Over there's Carmen Avenue. And that's...okay, let's go this way.

They turned down a wider lane of muddled stones. A burbling stream ran down the center of the street. The interconnected buildings were raised here on mossy stones, built from scrappy wooden paneling painted in a thick darkening gloss, with windows like rampart slits. A group of dirty children ran passed them, bare feet splashing in the water. A musty fog hung in the air: the visible odor of garbage and feces.

Koryn jumped across the stream and led Saul to a set of jagged stairs. She paused at a platform that branched to either side, took the more well-lighted of the two paths. She scurried down a corridor hung with threads of dank miasma like spider's webs. Another dark corridor gaped to their left and Koryn quickened her pace to reach the next set of stairs, a rickety-looking spiral staircase speckled with rust.

"They'll never find us up here," Koryn mumbled, mostly to herself.

"What do these people do?" Saul whispered.

"They sell things. Scavenged from the dumping grounds mostly. A few are really good at fixing things up. Or they just sell drugs."

Saul nodded.

"My mother always told me only scum lived in Luto's Court," Koryn said. "But you think they choose to live this way? Well...maybe, if you need a good place to hide..."

They came out on a walkway of wooden slats secured to a metal frame along a wall of doors spread every few feet. Leaning against the railing watching them was a man smoking a cigarette through a wooden cigarette holder. The man wore an uncolored trench coat several sizes too large for his hunched frame. His face was a mosaic of scars and lines that seemed to fill with the muggy smoke that hung about his face.

The man's slanted eyes watched them.

"Galen?" Koryn said.

The man flinched. Then he looked at Koryn more closely. "Koryn? What?" He looked at Saul, efficiently appraising his appearance. He bit down on his cigarette holder so the cigarette jittered dramatically. He nodded his head toward the nearest door. "You better step inside."

"Ja?"

"What, Ji?"

"I'm hungry."

"I knew you would be."

At one time the elevator has gone all the way to the top level but now leaves them still several levels beneath the surface, rumbling to a shuddering halt, dumping them in a corridor almost completely bereft of lighting. A strained electrical wire fizzes briefly, then leaves them in the dark. They grope up the spiraling stairwell.

"I believe it is the third ground level we're looking for. Keep an eye out, will you, Ji?"

"I'm so hungry I could eat a finger."

"Don't do that again, Ji. We'll reach our destination soon enough."

A faint square of light grows larger as they waddle up the creaking steps as fast as they can.

"Will there be things to eat, Ja?"

Ja smiles, showing his teeth to the gloom. "Oh, yes. I believe there will be. Plenty for us both."

The dream fades and is forgotten...

"So you're looking for your son?"

Saul nodded.

They sat on the floor in what appeared to be a tiny motel room. A small table lay pushed against one wall, a forlorn dresser against another. In the far corner—the room's only chair—was a collapsed recliner, an ugly green color scuffed with grime. A thin, door-less opening looked into a tiny bathroom saturated in moldy yellow tones.

"Have you seen him?" Saul asked. "My son? I've come a long way to find him."

Galen gave him a careful look. "Perhaps."

His heart was beating very quickly. "What do you know?" Saul asked.

"First, tell me—you come from downriver?"

"Yes."

Galen glanced sharply at Koryn, who nodded. He turned back to Saul. He sighed. "I don't know much. All I can tell you is that I've seen him, I think. Young. Light hair. Maybe seven or eight years old."

"He's nine."

"Yes, okay. The boy I saw could have been nine. But what struck me as odd, what makes me think he was your son, is the clothing he wore. A black t-shirt with an unusual print on the front of it, animals parading—"

"Yes!"

Galen shook his head. "I've dreamed about him then too. A small boy, wreathed in darkness."

Saul leaned forward, eager and restless. "Where did you see him?"

"In the heart of the city, with the shadow animals. They were taking him to the Theatre Verrata."

Koryn groaned.

"I'm sorry," Galen said.

Saul looked from Koryn then back to Galen. "How can I get him? Who are the shadow animals? The theatre what? How can I take him back home?"

Galen looked intently at his hands, silent for a time, until Saul was just about to say something, and he spoke. "It may be too late."

"Too late?" Saul said. "Too late for what?"

Koryn said, "There's only one reason your son would be in the Theatre Verrata." She looked saddened.

Galen nodded. "It's too bad."

Saul put his hands up. "Wait a minute. What are you saying? Just show me where my son is so I can take him back. I'll use this if I have to," he said, raising the rifle. "Just tell me where to go."

Koryn turned to Saul, put her hands on his shoulders, and fixed her liquid-brown eyes on his. "It's impossible. You can't get into that place."

"Then what am I supposed to do?"

There was a crash as the door split open. A hulking form hunched in the doorway. "You come with us, pretty-kitty."

"Yes, Ji, I believe that's right. It would be best if you came with us, sir. It would be best, mostly assuredly, for everyone, if you came quietly."

Saul gaped from the floor; they were talking to *him* he realized. Koryn was on her feet in an instant. Galen began to stand.

The form was bulbous and asymmetrical. It stood on bare muscular legs, with a broad hunchbacked abdomen draped in tattered scraps of clothing, from which protruded one human-looking arm and one oversized appendage like a writhing, many-joined spider. A huge, slobbering mouth with teeth and twitching lips formed a parody of a smile from the center of the form's stomach. An elongated neck jutted from the top, with round and colorless eyes shining from within a substance like dark mist, an immaculately polished bowler hat floating atop, which the human arm lifted to Saul in an ironic gentleman's gesture.

"He looks tasty, Ja. All of them look soooo good."

"Not this gentleman, Ji. He must arrive unspoiled." The normal arm reached out, beckoning to Saul. "If you'd come with us, please, sir."

Saul stared. "What? I—"

"He's not going anywhere." Koryn, in an instant taking a fighting stance, came forward. She held—flashing into her fingers from the fold of her coat—what appeared to Saul to be a pair of metallic chopsticks in each hand, their four points glistening wickedly in the yellow glow from the open bathroom.

Saul felt numb, as if mired in a dream.

Ja and Ji stepped into the room, almost casually. Koryn dove, skidding easily beneath Ji's clumsy swing, her needles stabbing, then rending flesh in a rusty spray across the floor. She spun, came around; the needle weapons flashed again and dark holes of brimming blood opened along the back of Ja's shoulder and down his spine.

Koryn crouched by the collapsed recliner, her weapons at the ready for another strike. "That's poison," she said.

Ja and Ji turned to face her. "We know."

"I can feel it! I can feel it!" Ji said.

Blood dribbled as the brother's smiled.

Galen took a step forward. "Wait, Koryn, don't—"

Koryn came again, taking a low stance; her needles flashed, opening more holes in the brother's flank, but Ji's hand was fast this time, striking like a snake, catching Koryn about the neck, lifting her, drawing her in. Koryn thrashed, her face already an ugly purple. She drove her needles, with all her strength, into Ji's flesh. The needles sunk into the soft muscle like cheese. Ji never flinched.

Koryn sputtered, her arms dropped; she sagged.

Galen pushed Saul toward the bathroom, began to back away.

Ji's mouth gibbered with anticipation. He lifted Koryn, and there was a snap, as he took her leg in his mouth, and began to crunch and mumble. "Mm...sooooo good..."

Galen was screaming something, but Saul was fascinated, couldn't tear his horrified eyes away.

Blood sprayed in a brownish geyser, as Ji reached Koryn's abdomen. There was a horrible hissing noise, as organs were loosened and separated from their functioning locations, flesh pulled from bone, and the farting sound of escaping gases, as the stomach was forced out, ugly and wet, between the splitting rib cage.

"Now, Mr. Saul, please. Come with me," Ja said, even as Ji continued to eat.

With a wet, smacking sound, a heavy string of viscera tumbled to the floor all at once.

Galen yelled in his ear. Ja stepped toward him. Ji dropped the half-consumed Koryn to the floor reluctantly, his tongue flopping out of his mouth and reaching for the remains with longing as his brother pulled him toward Saul.

Ja stared at him intently, continued to talk. "He'll come with us now, Ji."

"But I'm still hungry, Ja."

"I know, Ji. I know."

Saul felt something at his back: the crumbling wall. He was trembling. The only place left to go was into the cramped bathroom.

Galen came forward, putting himself between Saul and the brothers.

"This is not your concern, Galen," Ja said. "Please step aside."

"Go, Saul," Galen said, turning his head, his cigarette holder still clenched between his teeth, cigarette still smoldering.

Saul looked into the tiny bathroom. "Where?"

The brothers crossed the room. Ji smiled hungrily at Galen. Ja's eyes sparkled.

"In the back. Go!" Galen shoved him and Saul fell against the toilet. He groped his hands over the wall, lifting himself. He could feel his fingers being cut on the flaking paint.

"You better come with us too, Galen. You're an exiled criminal."

Galen shoved him again and the wall gave beneath Saul's shoulders. Saul reeled into a dark corridor.

"Go! Go!" Galen said.

Saul ran down the thin, single-file corridor, Galen breathing right behind him. They came to a rickety set of spiraling stairs. Saul glanced back. Ja and Ji stood in the bathroom at the end of the corridor, too large to squeeze through, Ja's darkness writhing and Ji licking his lips. In the pale yellow light of the bathroom, they looked ghostly and dead. Then the brothers turned to find another way around, and disappeared from view.

* * *

Galen flicked a match to light. They were somewhere dark, subterranean.

"She helped me...she..."

"Quiet, Saul. You have to be quiet. I'll tell you when you can talk."

Saul followed the pinpoint flame, a flickering sprite dancing ahead in the total dark. When he glanced away, faded copies of the sprite cavorted before his eyes.

The flame stopped. Saul could just make out the side of Galen's face, his concave eye, his scar-crossed cheek. The strange man was passing the flame over something on the wall. He brushed cobwebs and grime from the face of a control panel of some sort. He looked carefully for a minute or two.

"Where are we going?"

Galen shushed him, and then pulled something on the wall. Saul heard the dull hum of electricity being generated and there was the squealing sound of old machinery shuddering to life. Galen waited. The machinery crunched, then ceased. The electrical hum continued.

"Damn." Galen began to pound his fists lightly over the wall. The flame sprite went out. Saul could hear Galen struggling, breathing heavily, pushing his weight against the wall. Then, there was a rusty scraping noise, and the panel of a door slid open, revealing a faint glow of orange light. Saul felt a hand wrap his jacket, and pull him forward.

Inside, there was a cramped space, a tiny square room. In one corner there was a moldering heap of blankets. A few flies buzzed lethargically in the rotten heat. A lone chicken leg with a single bite torn from it lay near the door. Somewhere distantly above, whined an electric light.

Galen slid the door closed and tried the control panel next to it. At first he pushed the buttons lightly, but then began to mash them with his fists. When nothing happened, he stopped.

"We'll wait here," Galen said. "I was hoping this shaft still worked, but..." He shrugged. "There's another way, but it's too dangerous right now. They'll be looking for us."

"They killed her," Saul said, his voice shaking.

"Yes."

"They...oh my god...my god..."

"What's after you, Saul?"

"I—don't know."

"Why is it chasing you?"

Saul shook his head.

"You have to go home. It's too dangerous."

Saul choked back a sob. "I can't..."

Galen sighed. "I know. I'll help you—in what ways I can. Just be quiet for now."

Saul cried, unable to restrain his worries and his tensions any longer, but quietly into his hands, watching Galen fit his cigarette holder with a fresh cigarette and light it, the tiny flaring ember, the pale light, the scars on Galen's face, eyes glimmering in darkness.

It was when I first began going on camping trips upriver with my son—just like my father did with me, because he would want me to do the same with my son— that I started to wonder about the Copperton Forest. As a kid, I'd never thought to question the great furry rodents the size of sheep that sometimes grazed in the shade beneath the trees, or the flightless three-foot-tall auks waddling along the water's edge, or the tangle vines that I saw, on more than one occasion, snatch birds right out of the air as they flew by; and as an adult, dull and dismissive to wonder, I'd forgotten and never travelled far. But my inquiries were met with shrugs and shaking heads. When I eventually went to the library—the voice of my father in my head again—the only book I was able to find, the only written information of any real value, was Gately's brief entry in Unusual Landscapes.

Even so, my son and I never, on those initial trips, made it as far as the village of Sage, and it is never mentioned in the Gately text. I wonder if things would have been different if we had. Could my son have made friends there? Would they have known him and protected him? Or was the darkness, as alluring as a sweet yet poisonous cloud, already too great?

Perhaps I should have known then, that when the floods came that year, as the rains came every year, they would be the great ones. A "One-hundred-year Flood," they called it. I should have known that year, that when the waters came, when they were particularly violent, when they filled the arroyo by my house, crept up the bank and over the flood walls as I'd only seen happen once before when I was very young, they came with purpose.

"Alright, let's go," Galen said.

"Where?"

Galen stood in the dark corridor, turned his head up slowly so that the glow from his cigarette illuminated his face, smiled crazily. "Follow me."

Saul stepped after his new guide.

They moved quickly through a cramped hallway of dirt-caked tile, turned a corner and were in a vast area, in darkness that echoed. The sound from the padding of their shoes through the grit came back to them, as if they were being followed. Then, abruptly, they were in another corridor and there was the softness of daylight ahead. Galen was pushing on something and a door opened and they were outside and it was too bright to see. Saul squinted and held his hands over his eyes.

"They won't bother you in this part of the city," Galen was saying. "At least, not as long as you're with me."

Slowly, Saul's eyes adjusted to the daylight. Galen was watching him somberly, his smile completely wiped away, so that it seemed as if it'd never been, and perhaps it hadn't.

"They won't find us in broad daylight?" Saul asked.

"Well, since the lift I wanted to use seems to be out of commission, this is the best possible way to get around." A hint of a smile twitched Galen's lips for a moment, then was gone. "Come on."

Saul followed Galen around some piled up sacks of trash and down the alleyway. They were swept into the crowd moving slowly through the busy street and Saul's senses were instantly overwhelmed. Everywhere there were people in funny hats and clothing and they all seemed to be talking at once. A woman in a grand flowing dress approached, the bodice of her gown opened to allow her bare breasts free to the air, tiny green birds flitting about within. A man thrust sticks of meat into their faces, screaming, "Curried meats! Curried meats!" A tiny boy winked at him from between the legs of a woman of almost paper-white skin, her hair styled to appear as if it were whipped cream. A gruff looking man smoked a small pipe and made exaggerated expressions of surprise and awe with his face. From deep within the crowd, a hairless man of perhaps nine feet in height moved with the people, his skin tinged a faint purple color.

Galen drew him into the current and they walked. "This," Galen proclaimed, "is the aptly named Merchant Street."

Saul was stunned and didn't know what to say.

"We don't have far to go, but, as you can see, it's rather slow moving. You can be sure, however, we'll be safe here. Just watch your pockets carefully."

Saul pulled his pack tight over his shoulders, suddenly self-conscious. As long as they moved with the people, they didn't seem to have any trouble getting around.

"I'm afraid," Galen said, "my conversational skills are somewhat lacking. I've spent too much time alone in recent years. Perhaps I could tell you a story? Or catch you up on the latest city rumors?"

51

Saul stared at a cart piled high with bodies, flies buzzing about, sitting to the side, dripping blood in the street.

"Did you know, just last week, there was supposed to be a sighting of Marrow's Aerial?"

Saul tore his eyes away from the cart of bodies. "What?"

"It's just a rumor, of course, and you've probably never heard of it, but Marrow's Aerial is said to be a great flying ship, sometimes glimpsed amongst the clouds. Upon its prow sits a giant stone totem, an elongated head with cavernous eyes and an open mouth with a great fire forever burning within; and it is this totem which propels the ship, fed on the burning of books. And so, because of this, Marrow's Aerial is also a great library, with shelves upon shelves of tomes old and new, most mundane, but some of exquisite rarity, from worlds beyond reckoning and antiquity, and from civilizations ancient and forgotten."

Ahead of them, the crowd parted and there was a cluster of kids circling a man's cart piled high with animal cages. It was impossible to see the exact nature of the animals through the tightly-spaced bars, but, as Saul watched, a tiny pink hand reached out and, with a quick swipe, scratched a little boy on the nose. The boy jerked back with a hiss and the man whose cart it was screamed at the kids, "Get away! Get away!"

Unable to remove his eyes from the spectacle around him, Saul heard himself ask Galen, "Who are you?"

"I'm Galen! Haven't you heard of me? Although I've gone by other names. I'm the prophet, but I forget you're not from around here."

Further ahead, people brandished wooden poles with dark leathery things stretched into crosses at their tips. "The prophet?" Saul asked.

"Yes. I'm the model for the prophet Galen. At least I was originally, before my disfigurement. My original name was Randolph—my friends called me Randy. When I still had friends, that is." They walked by a troupe of dancers spinning shawls about their bodies like mist. "When I was young, with no idea what to do with my life, I fell asleep drunk one day in the streets after a night of whoring, and when I awoke, found myself in a factory of sorts, surrounded by plastic molded copies of myself. I fled. Soon, my likeness began to spring up all over the city, my own eyes staring back at me from the spires of buildings and the tops of towers. Tiny versions of me were being sold in the streets. They still are!" Galen laughed. "I was rather good looking back in those days, don't you think?" He pointed to a building not far from them that looked like a church. At the top of the stairs that led up to it, there stood a life-size figure of a young man with dark hair and a discerning look, his arms crossed, dressed in rags.

"Doesn't look anything like you," Saul said.

Galen sighed. "Not now, no. A prophet for the common people they called me, still call their memory of me. Now I'm old, and they prefer to remember me as I was. Even my dreams, that once so accurately foretold the future, betray me now."

Saul didn't know what to say. "I'm sorry."

"It's not your concern. See there?" Galen pointed down the street directly ahead of them, which was now thinning of people, the merchants less densely packed. "See that tower, the tallest one?"

Saul looked. A narrow column shot up from what appeared to be a small city park. Higher than all the other buildings around it, it might have been made from stone, dusted with green moss in places, sanded smooth.

"Your son's in there," Galen said. "The Theatre Verrata. At the very top. Yet there's no direct entrance."

Saul swallowed, felt for his rifle strapped to his pack. "How do I get inside?"

"Some say there are great riches at the top of the Theatre Verrata, or great truths. Some try to scale its height, but none have made it, I don't believe. They either fall or are shot down by snipers from one of the adjacent buildings."

"Then what do you suggest I do?"

Galen looked at Saul gravely, appraising. "I like you," he said. "You remind me of myself a little, in a way. I'll continue to help you. We go under."

"Under?"

"Of course. I've spent most of my adult life living in the labyrinth beneath the City. I know a way that has long been forgotten." Catching him off guard, Galen leaned in close and smiled like Saul had seen him smile only once before in the shadows. "But I found it," he said, then the smile was gone. "I'll take you there."

Galen turned down one of many narrow alleys. Saul followed him until he stopped. "Alright," he said. "We'll start here." He pointed to a circular manhole cover set in the pavement. "Into the sewers we go."

I killed her. I should have done something. I should have stopped her.

Somehow, going into the darkness and the dampness beneath the city brought a bitter ache to my heart. I could see her in front of me, before my eyes adjusted to the lack of light, dangling, her face shocked, accusing, even as her internal parts dribbled and flopped to the concrete. I'd known her only a very short time, but she felt, at that moment, like a daughter to me. She could have been my *daughter. I could have taken care of her, would have been glad for the responsibility, would have worked twice as hard to feed an extra mouth at home. I could see her sitting across the kitchen table, Ezzy slurping spaghetti next to her, my wife smiling at them both.*

We crept in silence along the dank walkway, the water in the canal sliding by next to us, things scurrying and making rustling sounds all around.

We walked for a long time. I don't know how long. Until, eventually, we came to a place where light spilled down upon us through lazily spinning fans from grates far above. We sat in one of the small alcoves, an unremarkable wall of brick on one side. Galen said we had to wait. For what, he wouldn't say.

Despite the light far above, it was very dark. I couldn't make out Galen's face as he spoke now for the first time since we'd left the surface. He told me a story while we waited. A creation story.

"Do you know of Awa?" Galen asked me, seemingly from nowhere.

I shook my head—I'd never heard the term.

"Before the material world existed, and everything that we know to be the earth and sky, there was only the Void." Galen's voice was quiet, nearly a whisper. "Awa, a presence passing by the Void, became distracted by a sound. It was faint, this sound, but, having never experienced the sensation of hearing, Awa stopped to investigate. Fascinated by the sound, Awa discovered It could make sound as well and began to compose music. Awa composed the first harmonies, the first lilting waves that began to reveal hints of a greater reality beneath. Awa then created a huge mountain, so that It would have a place to play Its music. Awa then began to create things around this mountain, to give the mountain an orientation of importance in relation to the earth below. Awa created the physical lands, the trees, the ground, and then the animals and the birds. Atop the mountain, It created all manner of apparatuses for the production of sound.

"Then, in order to fully experience that which It had created, to satisfy Its curiosity, Awa created a physical form for Itself. Awa discovered life was wonderful, filled with pleasures, bodily and spiritual—from the warmth of the Comet It had created, to the flavor of food and drink, to the sheer joy of the imagination and creation. But life, Awa also discovered, was filled with much pain. Awa became aware of the burden of time, that nothing It created seemed to last, that no form of life seemed capable of living forever. Awa created companions for Itself, in Its own image, in order to allay the agony of loneliness, and created the pleasure of sex as a way to know his new companions intimately, then later as a means of self-

56

perpetuating creation, so that degenerating life might live on and on. Awa began to age and experience Its own degeneration.

*   "Awa created all manner of things to ease Its aching body. It created vast comforts to balance the displeasures It had somehow created as well. And when It was too old to lift Its feebly failing body, Awa lay down at the top of Its mountain and looked out into the Void and wondered if their were others like It, somewhere out there. Then Awa remembered the sound It had first heard, that faint voice, and finally understood what it had said, a single word,* The Word: *'Death.'"*

*   Galen fell silent for a time, and we sat in the dark without speaking, while I pondered his story.*

*   That's how he told it, the best I can remember.*

*   Yet, still, even after that, I couldn't get Koryn's death—she never even had a chance to scream—out of my head.*

After what could have been hours or days, Galen lifted his head. "It's nearly dark now," he said.

Saul cleared his throat. "Is that what we're waiting for?"

"Yes. And the beam."

"The beam?"

"Just watch," Galen said, staring intently at the brick wall beneath which they huddled.

Saul watched, the light from above fading, the alcove darkening even more. "What are—?"

Galen hushed him with a raised hand.

Saul sighed and fixed his eyes on the wall, trying to locate the spot in which Galen seemed to be so interested. After a couple of minutes, a faint mark of light began to crawl up the wall, brightening as it travelled. Galen was crouched now; Saul could sense his tense muscles, ready for something.

When the light was nearly halfway up the wall, it suddenly flared, and Galen leapt into action, thrusting something he held in his fist, that Saul hadn't noticed him take from his coat, into the light.

Instantly, the wall shifted, and another black passage opened before them.

"A duskdoor," Galen said. "But you still have to have the key."

Galen shifted his cigarette holder, which he'd held tightly in the corner of his mouth the entire time they'd been walking, from one side of his mouth to the other. He flicked a match to life and held it out so Saul could see the opening was only a small and featureless room. When the flame on his match had nearly reached his finger, he used it to light his cigarette, and dropped the match into the dark. He reached out and put the small box of matches in Saul's hand. Saul could still see the spot of flame pulsing before his eyes.

"Inside," Galen said, "there should be climbing rungs going up the wall. Be careful. They are very old."

Saul looked carefully at Galen. "You're not coming with me?"

"I can't help you any further, I'm afraid. At the top, you'll find your son, inside the Theatre Verrata."

Saul tucked the matches into his pocket. He shrugged. "You've gotten me this far." He stepped into the small room, began feeling the cold and crumbling walls for the rungs Galen was talking about.

"You're fortunate to have found me," Galen said. "You might even make it out of this alive. Not every meeting is a coincidence."

Saul found the rungs and began to climb. He looked down, and saw Galen's face poked into the room looking up at him, his cigarette appearing in the dark to float before his face. "How is all of this here?" Saul asked, his mind reeling suddenly through the things he'd seen.

Galen smiled, for the third time that day, and then, without an answer, pulled his head out of sight, and Saul's life forever.

* * *

Saul was alone again. It was very quiet. He moved carefully, lifting each hand in turn, feeling for the next

59

rung, making sure it wasn't loose or so rusted it might cut his skin, then pulling himself up and on to the next one. He could see nothing, although he could sense a light source above him. He could hear himself panting as he strained; he wasn't as young as he used to be. If he slipped, he was done, and he still had a very long way to go.

After a while, he began to wonder at the height of the tower. It seemed as if he'd been climbing for a very long time. He tried to bring to mind how the tower had looked when he'd seen it from the outside. Approximately how many stories would he say it was? Ten? Twenty? Below him, there seemed to be a vast emptiness; above, a thickening darkness that pushed on his shoulders and the top of his head. His backpack was very heavy. He should have left some of his belongings at the bottom, only taken his rifle.

Something scuttled below him.

Saul froze, his heart suddenly beating with fear, suddenly aware of the sweat running down the side of his face, tickling his lower back, slicking the space between the palms of his hands and the corroded metal rungs he gripped for dear life. He tried to hold his breath and listen, but doing so only made his breathing harder, more ragged. Something moved in the shadows below him and he thought of Ja and Ji, that huge gibbering mouth and those maliciously intelligent eyes shining out at him, that ridiculous bowler hat. He realized, only too late, that he'd been so stunned by the sights around him he'd forgotten the danger he was in, the relentless agents of what pursued him. He'd allowed himself to be mystified by Galen's stories, to forget for a moment why he was here, what he was doing. He'd forgotten about the presence that wanted him, that wanted his son.

He forced himself to move more quickly. He tried to imagine the ponderous form of Ja and Ji climbing the ladder and decided, if they *were* able to climb, they would not be able to climb faster than he could. And he had a head start. He concentrated on the rungs, one hand at a time, end over end. He moved, all too aware of his rifle, smacking his hip with each upward step.

Slowly, he realized he could see the ladder rungs, faintly protruding from the old brick wall. And he could see his hands, white smudges moving in front of him. He began to move with renewed confidence; he was approaching the top.

Another sound echoed up to him from below. A voice? Whispered words? A grunt of effort?

Saul, nearly out of breath, his muscles hot and wobbly, glanced upward. There was an opening, a small square of light. Below him: a clanking sound, and the wall seemed to shudder. He put his eyes on the light and continued to climb, faster and faster as the light drew closer.

It was a hatch in the floor, he saw, nearly there. It was open and pale, greenish light shone from within.

Oooo! Hungry! So hungry!

Saul nearly screamed. He bit his lip and flung himself upward. The straps on his backpack dug into his shoulders, the stock of his rifle bruised his hipbone; he reached through the opening. His hand fumbled for purchase. He pulled himself up, his feet dangling and vulnerable in the dark below. His backpack caught on the edge; the opening was too narrow for him and his backpack to fit through at the same time. He could see Ji's massive, segmented hand reaching for his feet, catching one, ripping his foot free of his leg with an effortless *sploosh* of blood. He pulled, with all his strength, wedged in the opening. That mouth of mismatched teeth trembling with anticipation. He kicked out, his foot finding nothing: empty space. He kicked again and his foot caught on one of the rungs and he pushed with everything he had. He pushed through, scrambling over the floor. He fumbled with his backpack, trying to free his rifle. He rolled over onto his stomach. He ripped his rifle free and turned it to face the proper direction and set the butt in his shoulder and pointed the barrel at the opening, waiting for Ja's head to rise up so he could blow him away.

He waited.

Nothing came up. He must have stared at the opening for several minutes, until his eyes became dry and itchy and he was forced to blink. He must have imagined what he'd heard; being alone in the dark had been terrifying, had played tricks with his mind.

Slowly, he became aware of the room surrounding him. Its greenish hue from the glowing lights, its small and circular dimensions, the many things painted all across its walls. He sat up and looked around.

His son was sitting quietly on the other side of the room, turned away from him, staring up at one of the murals.

"Ezzy!" He ran to his son, grabbed him around the shoulders and hugged him, held him out so he could look into his son's face.

Ezzy looked back, blinking, clearly stunned; he smiled vaguely.

Saul hugged his son, squeezed him tight, never wanted to let go. "Are you alright, Ezzy? Are you okay? Did they hurt you?"

"I'm okay."

Saul clutched his son. "Yes you are. Thank god." He ran his fingers through his son's hair.

"Daddy?" Ezzy said, his voice muffled against Saul's chest.

"Yes?"

"I knew you were coming."

"Of course you did. I could never let them take you."

"They showed me. Look."

"Yeah? That's great, that's—" Saul stopped, one the wall paintings had caught his eye. It depicted an old man with a backpack slung over his shoulders hugging a little blonde boy, and he knew the old man was him and the blonde boy his son.

"Everyone sees different things."

Saul wheeled about. Because the room was circular, and there was no clear beginning, his eyes didn't know where to begin. He took in images that were highly recognizable. One was of his son surrounded by the shadowy silhouettes of animals. Another was of him looking up at a young woman with dark hair—Koryn—in a tree. Another showed Galen pointing to a statue of himself. Another showed his wife sick in bed. Another showed Ezzy climbing up the outside of the Theatre Verrata. Another showed Merchant Street filled with water. And he was about to go around again to see all of the images he'd missed, when he came back to the painting of him hugging his son. Behind them, in the painting, coming out of the hatch in the floor, was a shape ugly and dark—with a bowler hat perched atop its head.

Saul turned and thrust his son away. He'd left the rifle lying on the floor and he groped for it blindly.

"A pretty kitty, Ja! Such a pretty kitty!"

"I do believe you mean Ezzy," Ja said. "A pretty Ezzy."

The brothers climbed through the opening, Ji's massive hand raking the floor for purchase.

"I'm so hungry, Ja."

"I know, Ji, but these ones are to be taken alive, I'm afraid."

Saul kicked out, sliding on the floor.

"What about their arms? They don't need those, do they?"

"No, I suppose not, but, well...we'll see."

The brothers moved on Saul, arms raised.

Saul grabbed the rifle, lifted it, and fired. The shot caught the brother's in the abdomen, blood splattering and beginning to flow, but without effect; they moved over him without slowing.

Saul kicked out again, sliding away, raised the rifle, and pulled the trigger again. *Click*. Nothing.

"Yes, Ji, I suppose. Just his arms."

Saul grunted. One had to cock the rifle, to release the spent shell and reload an unspent one from the magazine into the chamber.

"Please don't give us any trouble, Mr. Saul, sir."

Saul pulled on the bolt handle, lifted the rifle, aimed. Ji's hand reached for him.

Saul pulled the trigger. This time, the shot was deafening, and the brothers staggered back. Immediately, they came for him again, but Saul jammed the bolt handle back and fired, and then he jammed it back, and fired again. He screamed. He fired and fired. He didn't even know how many shots his rifle held. All he knew was how to fire *his* rifle. He thought of all those times his father had mocked him for being a sissy. He fired *his* rifle again, and this time he saw the shot take Ja in his smoky face, and he grinned.

Ja and ji teetered at the edge of the opening in the floor.

Saul grabbed the bolt handle with his hand and slammed it back. He felt the hot shell casing burn his leg as it flew free, heard it strike the floor. He felt the fresh round enter the chamber, sliding snugly into place. He thought of what Ja and Ji had done to Koryn. He aimed his rifle. He fired.

The bullet struck Ji in the mouth, shattering teeth and gums. The brother's fell backward, caught themselves at the opening, Ji's segmented hand clinging to the floor.

Saul aimed again. He pulled the trigger. *Click.* Nothing.

The brother's began to pull themselves up. Ji's giant tongue snaked out and began to greedily lick its own blood and teeth down its throat. Ja's human-looking hand came up and wagged a scolding finger at Saul, as if to tell him he'd been bad, as one might a puppy that has just piddled on the rug.

Saul pulled the bolt handle again, but he knew his rifle was spent. There were extra bullets in his pack, but he didn't have time to find them and reload his rifle.

The brothers were nearly to their feet.

"Bastards!" Saul bit down on his lip and jumped to his feet. He no longer cared for his own safety. He ran to the brothers and began wildly beating them with the butt of his rifle.

"Please, Mr. Saul. That's unwise."

He smashed that bowler hat into that squiggling mass. The brother's slipped and fell. He smashed, again and again. Out of the corner of his eye, he saw Ji's large segmented hand coming around for him. He turned, and smashed the hand. He stomped on it with his boot and mashed the tips of those fingers as if they were the heads of snakes. Then he turned and began to smash the teeth from Ji's gums.

Ji said something, but his words were garbled with blood and sticky matter.

And then the brothers fell, no longer able to support themselves over the opening in the floor, and plummeted into darkness. They didn't scream and there was no sound of them falling. Only silence.

Saul backed away from the hole, and dropped his rifle to the floor. He wiped blood from his face with the back of his hand.

When he looked up, his son was standing on the other side of the room smiling at him. "Very good, Daddy! Very good!"

The only way out of the Theatre Verrata was down the same way I'd come up. I coached Ezzy, as best I could, trying not to show him how scared I was, but he didn't seem to have any trouble with the rungs—or the darkness. He went down silently, patiently; I assumed he was so stunned by what he'd been through, by what he'd seen—I know I was, and still am—that he was in survival mode, numb to his emotions. I didn't want to think about how different he was, changed somehow. I was too terrified by what we might find when we got to the bottom, what the mangled corpse of Ja and Ji would look like, what trauma it would cause my son, or, even more horrifying, that the brothers had somehow survived the fall, and would be waiting for us.

But when we reached the bottom, there was nothing. All traces of Ja and Ji had vanished. Perhaps the substance they'd been made from, the swirling matter that had composed Ja's face, had consumed them, or dissipated into the air, and been banished to the ether.

I remembered perfectly the way out and moved quickly. Ezzy followed easily, without protest—silently.

When we reached the streets, it was raining, a violent downpour that soaked us instantly, caused our clothing to cling to our bodies, dragging at our shoulders. My backpack became heavy and burdensome. My rifle swung by my side. I hadn't bothered to reload, hadn't considered it. Its stock struck the bruised spot on my hip painfully, but I ignored it.

Merchant Street was empty. Everywhere things huddled beneath tarps. Above us and to our sides, the windows in the buildings were closed, the shades drawn shut. As far as we could tell, we were alone. We moved as quickly as we could, avoiding the spots where the water pooled, or where the ground had become slick mud.

I brought us straight to the alley where Galen had led me, although it looked no different than any of the others, and into the dark tunnels again. I have always had an excellent sense of direction—it's one of the few qualities of mine my father actually admired—and I knew I could take us back the way we had come. I was still grateful, however, on several occasions, to have the matches Galen gave to me, slightly damp but still strike-able, tucked neatly in my pocket.

Suffice to say, I was able to lead us out, back through Luto's court—as boarded up and empty as Merchant Street—back the way I'd come, back through the secret entrance Koryn had shown me, to the other side of the Great Wall, and into the forest, where it continued to rain and I knew we needed to move as quickly as possible and find shelter and food. The yearly storm had come, and with it, so would the floods.

Saul moved miserably through the trees, pushing his feet through the slushy ground. Behind him, Ezzy followed. His son didn't appear to be experiencing the same discomfort as him, at least he wasn't showing it outwardly, his face calm, his eyes sparkling. Perhaps his son had been confined to that windowless room in the Theatre Verrata for so long he now relished the freedom of the outdoors, the feel of the rain pouring through the trees, the wind lashing at their exposed faces. Saul knew he had to find Sage—Koryn's village—and a place where they could stop and rest. He knew they couldn't continue this way for long.

Koryn had talked very little about her village, but had, when Saul had asked her about it, pointed out its general vicinity. He knew in which direction to go. The problem was how quickly the ground everywhere had become swampy, leaves and pine needles drifting like scum over the surface of pools that hid their depths, becoming deeper with each passing minute. And the light was already fading from the sky; they had little time to reach their destination.

With each step, his backpack grew heavier, the bruise on his hip larger. He kept asking Ezzy if he was doing all right. "Are you okay, son?" And Ezzy kept saying he was. "Yes, Daddy." They trudged on.

When the forest began to lose its color, becoming shadowy and indistinct, Saul became desperate. He grabbed Ezzy's hand and drove him on. He splashed through the murk, moving quickly and recklessly. Ezzy didn't say a word, trying to keep up. But when even Saul had to admit they were not going to make it to Sage before nightfall, he began to look for somewhere to hole up for the night, a spot of higher ground, anything.

When he saw the tree, a large and massive thing, he thought of Koryn, and how easily she'd swung through the branches. He thrust his son toward it. They climbed, Ezzy easily reaching and pulling himself up, Saul with more difficulty, the pack weighing him down, his exhaustion nearing the collapsing point. When they reached a large cluster of snaking branches, Saul slumped into them, letting them cradle his weight. He slipped his arms free of the backpack and found a comfortable position. He hugged his son tight, and slept, despite the cold and the roaring of the storm and the splashing rain on his face.

He dreamed of dark things and his son and many other things that, when he awoke, left vague and bitter foreboding like extra weight over his shoulders, memories lost yet their marks lingered.

* * *

In some places, the water now reached their knees and flowed against their legs in swirling eddies and cross-streams. Saul's feet ached and his lower back was a constant hot spot of pain. Ezzy stumbled and Saul had to catch him on several occasions. They were near the river now; the water flowed toward it. Saul moved now because he had no other choice. He had to get his son to safety. There was no other option. The direction in which Sage lay had been pointed out to him, but never its distance from the river.

Somehow, they moved up a slope, to a place where the water no longer tugged at the bottoms of their feet like sticky mud. The rain continued to batter them, but they began to move a little more easily and without having to trudge through pools of water. Everywhere the trees bent and groaned. Looking ahead, the rain was like a mist, a constant blurring of the landscape.

There was a building at the top of the next rise.

Saul squinted into the rain, blinking back the water. He took Ezzy's hand in his own and stomped forward. It was a squat cabin. It seemed a perfect addition to the forest, although also out of place somehow. Yet it had to be real. They must have finally reached the village of Sage.

After days of never-ending rain, Saul had almost become used to it. "You see that, Ezzy?" he screamed to be heard over the roar. "It's a cabin! We've made it!"

Ezzy smiled, nodded his head.

"Let's run, okay?"

Gripping Ezzy's hand tight, Saul began to bound up the slope. Ezzy followed easily. The sight of the cabin had renewed his energy; they were going to be okay.

When they reached the top of the rise, Saul let go of his son's hand and they raced to the cabin. Ezzy reached it first, slapping his hand on the rough wooden wall, then Saul came right behind him, laughing. He clapped his son on his tiny shoulders and brought him in for a hug. He almost didn't notice his son wasn't laughing.

The cabin was small, no more than a storage shed, windowless. Walking around to the other side, there was a door. Saul tried the knob; it was unlocked. He turned back and looked down the rise. His son was already staring.

What they saw, was red.

How can I describe it? At first, I couldn't tell what I was looking at. It was like a painting, or one of those old faded photographs, bled an ugly sepia color. The village was small, maybe fifteen households of perhaps twenty to thirty buildings. Water from the rain formed crimson ponds in places. Windows were broken and doors swung and slammed against the sides of their houses. And there were things in the road, the single muddy road that wound through the village. I couldn't tell what those things were from this distance. All I knew, in that moment, was that there was blood everywhere, enough to stain the road, enough to splatter across the sides of the houses, enough to mingle with the storm waters, tinting them red.

A deep fear rose up in me then. This place was not safe. I had to get my son away from here, yet we needed a place to weather the storm. We also needed food and there would be food in one of the houses. I shuddered to think what else we might find.

I grabbed my son, more roughly than I intended, to pull him away from the horror, and shoved him toward the shed we'd found. For a moment, when I saw his face, I was filled suddenly with a deep cold, but I looked away quickly. I had not seen a smile on my son's face. And then we were inside the small cabin and, with a great relief, out of the rain.

We huddled there for hours, but we both knew the rains were not going to let up, not for days now, and we'd have to risk them again in the morning. I decided we should stay the night, despite our apparent danger. We found some old and musty horse blankets and striped out of our soggy clothes and dried ourselves the best we could, wrapped in their heavy musk. There was dry firewood in one corner of the shed and I was able to get a fire going. Smoke quickly filled the small cabin, but with the door open our watery eyes and scratchy throats were tolerable, and we began to warm ourselves.

It was a grain shed, we quickly discovered, and in one corner there was a barrel of dried corn kernels. In a pot over the fire, I boiled a large portion of corn to a soft gruel and we ate that along with the last of the dried nuts I had in my pack.

Warm and dry and somewhat comfortable for the first time in what felt like weeks, we stayed up past dark, later than we should have probably. As the sun set and the light faded from the day, I sat in the doorway, my naked body wrapped in those scratchy blankets, and watched the color fade from the village. I watched until I could no longer see the ponds of water were crimson, or the stains on the house walls. I watched until the houses became indistinct heaps. I watched until the dark consumed everything. I shuddered, and turned back to the fire.

My son, who must have seen me shudder and sensed I was afraid, then said, "It's already been here, Daddy. That thing that has been chasing you. It won't get you here. Not now."

In the morning, they packed up their stuff, put their clothes back on, stiff and still damp, and stepped once more into the rain. They walked numbly through the village. The things littering the road, the shapes Saul had seen the night before, were the dismembered body parts of the villagers. Hands. Legs. Fingers. Strewn innards like dead and soggy snakes. Saul knew now that his son had already seen such things, that his son was likely already traumatized by these sights. He now knew why his son was acting so strangely. He tried to lead Ezzy quickly through the village, but there was no use trying to get him not to look. It was too late for that. This was the way of the world.

When he saw a promising house, he left Ezzy to wait in the doorway, and went inside. He moved to the kitchen. Sitting at the table was a family of four, slumped in their chairs, arms up and resting on its surface, as if waiting for dinner to be ready, their necks torn and gray and stringy with pale tendons and dark veins, all four of their heads missing. He searched the cabinets, and found rice, and beans, and some rock-hard biscuit things. He also found some jerky. He packed up these things and left quickly.

"What did you find?" Ezzy asked him when they were back on the road again.

"Nothing. Some food," Saul replied.

Ezzy smiled slyly. "Good. That's good."

It was only after they'd left the village of Sage behind them and were foraging through the forest once more that Saul realized something. A stone in his gut. Out of all those villagers, all those severed limbs, he hadn't seen a single head; all of their heads had been missing.

* * *

The next two days felt like weeks, and were agonizing, but uneventful. They followed the now-raging river and the forest shrunk subtly around them; the trees became smaller. The ground became more solid, more real. They returned, somehow, on foot, to the world they'd always known.

As they came into forest they recognized as territory close to home, Saul began to move more quickly. "We're almost home, Ezzy! We're almost home!"

They dashed onward. Saul knew they were safe now and that knowledge renewed his vigor and gave him strength. When they came to one of the bridges that crossed the arroyo just up the way from their house, Saul gave a shout of joy. He took Ezzy's hand and they began to run.

Turning the corner, Saul could see their house, up on the hill at the point where the asphalt street came to an abrupt end, overlooking the usually dry arroyo now filled with white water.

* * *

"Helen!" Saul yelled, flinging the front door open, dropping his soggy backpack on the porch outside. "Helen! I did it! I brought our son home!"

He led Ezzy to the couch, sat him down. "It's going to be okay now. Everything's okay now. Do you need something to drink? I'll get you something to drink."

Saul sprung down the hall, unmindful of his soggy boots on the carpet, or his dripping clothes. He practically galloped to the bedroom. He flung the door open, and the breath caught in his throat, as he suddenly became aware of the smell.

Helen sat as he'd left her, in bed, her back against the wall, arms at her sides, head slumped between her shoulders. It was as if she hadn't moved, even to feed herself. It was as if she'd simply given up and died, days ago, and her flesh had begun to bloat.

Saul wheeled about, screaming silently. He fell back into the hallway and slammed the bedroom door. His numb legs moved him through the house and back to the living room, where his son looked up, and nodded.

"Don't go in...don't go..." Saul's lips flapped.

"It's okay, Daddy," Ezzy said, getting up from the couch, leading Saul now to lie on it. "It's okay."

Saul sunk into the couch, utterly exhausted. It was an effort even to lift his arms. He had to get up, though. He had to help his son.

And it was with these thoughts, he passed into sleep.

"Let him sleep, Ji."

"But I'm hungry, Ja. I'm so hungry."

"Oh, I know, Ji. But he's been through so much, don't you think?"

Saul lifts his head and he knows he is in a dream. Even so, it is a dream with such detail, the chirping of insects, the cool breeze of night, the dewy grass itching the side of his cheek where he lays. He is in a field and all around him there is darkness, nothing to be seen in any direction. The only thing he can see is a chair, empty and alone, like a throne, waiting for its king.

And then the sounds begin: snarls and grunts, a chattering warble, snorts and bellows, combining to become a braying roar.

Saul brings himself to his feet. Staring into the darkness, he can see movement. There are animals there, lurking in the shadows.

He takes a step back.

The braying roar becomes louder as the animals draw closer and closer.

And then his son steps from the darkness amongst the shadow animals and comes toward him and he is terrified.

"Don't you see how great this is?" Ezzy says, and begins to laugh.

His son's laugh joins those of the shadow animal's, becoming such a sound as Saul has never heard.

Saul cringes back. This is not his son.

Ezzy grins, stepping up to the chair. "Do you really think things happen the way you remember them, they way you want them to?"

Ezzy sits on the throne.

"I'm going to change the world."

Saul's own screams wake him.

Saul awoke and staggered from the couch and into the kitchen. He sat at the table, breathing heavily, his heart pounding in his chest. He stared out the window, watching the storm continue its downpour. Slowly, he realized he'd only been dreaming, and he began to calm.

The waters in the arroyo were beginning to rise above the initial flood walls. The flooding was going to be bad this year. People's homes were going to see water. The waters, Saul realized, might even reach his house, if they kept going like this. He'd have to go out there with some sandbags and see if he could strengthen the walls.

He stood, walked to the cabinets, grabbed a glass, and filled it with water from the tap. He drank, then realized how incredibly thirsty and he was and drank the entire glass, filled it again and drank more. His stomach rumbled, was struck by a sudden sharp pain, then subsided, and went away.

Ezzy? Where was Ezzy?

He staggered from the kitchen, realizing only then that he was still in his soaking wet clothes. He moved down the hallway. He stood before his bedroom, the door closed, and turned the knob. He pushed the door open.

His wife sat on the bed with Ezzy in her lap. When they saw Saul standing there they both looked up and smiled at him.

"Saul, thank god!" Helen said. "I'm so glad you're back!"

Saul came forward to hug them both. He squeezed them tight and they both squeezed him back. His heart warmed and he couldn't speak.

"See, Daddy," Ezzy said. "Look. She's not dead. She'll always be with us."

Over the next few days, we left the house as little as possible. We watched the rains come, watched the arroyo flood like a white water canyon, watched the waters strike the floodwalls and then creep over them. I went outside and I did what I could with the sandbags from the shed, spending an entire day creating another wall closer to the house, but there was little else I could do. We watched, the three of us—mother, father and son—huddled by the kitchen window as, within hours of my walls completion, the waters came up to it and began to lap against it, then over it. There was nothing more to be done.

I thought a lot in those stormy days about the Copperton Forest upriver, about what those people might think of the seemingly unending rains, about the things that might be washed away, the unusual things, later to be found downriver. I thought about the "great green mountain," that served as a barrier meant to keep people out, that I had someone managed to breach, of the wonders I had glimpsed on the other side. I thought about Koryn, who had so easily and innocently been my friend. I thought about Sage, that poor village, and knew then what the floods were for, why they came so fully that year—to cleanse, to wash it all away...

In our house we waited for those waters to reach us, to climb our walls, to clean the world of us—my wife, my son and me. We waited and we trembled.

But, this year was not the exception we feared, and, quite abruptly, the waters began to recede.

It happened, as it did every year: one morning I awoke to the chirping of birds. I got up and looked out the bedroom window and I could see sunshine. Excited, I shook my wife awake and told her to come and look. Groggily, she stood by my side, rubbing her eyes, but when I flung the shades back and the sunlight shone suddenly into our bedroom, she clutched me tight and smiled. "I told you not to worry," she said, rolling her eyes, and I laughed. I laughed like I hadn't laughed in what felt like a very long time.

I rushed down the hall to Ezzy's room, pushed his door open without knocking, and ran to his bed, but it was empty. "Ezzy!" I called out. "Ezzy! The sun's up! The storm is over!"

I rushed down the hall again and found him in my study. He was looking at all the things I'd collected from the storms of year's past, displayed on the shelves that lined the walls. He looked up at me as I burst into the room.

"Soon, Ezzy," I said. "The storm is over and soon you can go down to the arroyo and have a look. Who knows what you'll find this year!"

He looked at me and smiled a little, as he did a lot now. "Good, Daddy. That's good."

Saul awoke from another horrible nightmare. He'd been alone in the house because his wife was dead and her bloated body washed away during the flood and his son had run away upriver. And the unnamable thing that pursued him had found him, just as his father had said would happen.

He sat up, dropping his feet over the side of the bed. He clutched himself, sweat beading his forehead, the cool night air sending a shiver through his entire body. He stood, and walked slowly from the bedroom. He crossed the hall and to the kitchen. He ran himself a glass of water from the tap and drank.

His dream had shaken him badly, but, slowly, his heart began to calm and the fear began to recede, just as the floodwaters had done. He took his glass of water and walked down the hallway to his study. He was too awake now to go back to sleep and thought he'd read for a while.

He pushed the door open and stepped inside. He crossed to his desk, where there was a small lamp. He reached his hand out and flipped the lamp to life.

Something was behind him.

He turned, and, on the other side of the room, just below the strange map of the territory upriver, his son lay in the shadows.

It had finally found him, and began to unfurl.

EXCERPT FROM *GHOSTS OF EDEN*

Publication date: November 2014

KAYLA'S WEEKEND

ONE

She'd been promised the next book by this weekend—her friend from school, Stephanie, had said she would lend it to her—but now it was Saturday and she had nothing to do. She'd read the first five Narnia books eagerly, consuming them like rare nourishing fruit, then, picking the fruit pit clean, read them again and again. She was most excited by the next book, *The Magician's Nephew*, because Stephanie had told her it was about Professor Digory Kirke from the first book and the creation of Narnia and about stumbling into other worlds and...

"You know what I think?" her father said. "Hey. Wake up. I'm talking to you."

Kayla's head snapped up. She hadn't noticed her father had come into the living room and was staring at her intensely from the other side of the couch. His eyes were bloodshot, but he didn't stagger as he came forward, falling into his reclining chair.

"Why don't you go daydream somewhere else, is what I think. Play with your brother. The game's about to start."

It was Saturday and that meant it was the weekend and, as usual, as a way to make up for the long dry workweek, her father and mother had begun drinking at just before noon. They drank with a reckless dedication, each frosted bottle or sloshing inch of swirling treacle in a finger-smeared glass like a reward for the finishing the one before it.

Kayla turned to leave the living room.

"Hey," her father said. "That bottle of vodka in the freezer. Get it for me, will ya? Don't roll your eyes at me." He slumped back into the couch.

* * *

All afternoon, Kayla was restless. She felt strange. She tried to read for a while. *The Lion, the Witch, and the Wardrobe* was the only book she owned, but her eyes couldn't track the words, letters jittering on the page. She didn't know why she felt this way, like she was waiting for something to happen, as if she sensed something lurking beneath the surface of this dull afternoon, something insidious—and exciting.

At one point, she wandered into her brother's room.

The sounds of war immediately filled the room: gunfire and explosions and men yelling and screaming.

Without taking his eyes from the screen, Bradley said, "You wanna play?"

"Sure," Kayla said. She was bored enough.

But Bradley was a better player than her and laughed cruelly every time he killed her, blowing her head off with a plasma grenade or shooting her arms off so her character was helpless, running around like a chicken. And, after twenty minutes, she dropped the game controller to the floor and went to do something else.

"You suck," her brother said as she was leaving. "Big time."

* * *

While her parents watched television in the living room, Kayla made spaghetti, browning the meat, pouring over it a jar of marinara sauce as bright and red as blood. She called everyone to the table.

"How are you feeling, Mom?"

Her mother let out a snort. "Stupid child. Just leave me alone."

Kayla felt her heart leap, as if slapped, but was careful not to show how much her mother's words stung her.

They ate in silence. Kayla looked from one face to the other. Bradley and her father ate quickly, while her mother moved her fork around absently. Her parent's faces looked puffy, more strained around the eyes than usual.

"Finished?" her father asked her mother.

Her mother shook her head, as if from a doze. "Yes. Yes, of course."

Her father snatched their mother's nearly untouched bowl and, along with his own empty one, took them into the kitchen, tossing them in the sink with a clatter. "Come on, Laura," he said when he came back, taking her mother's arm. He led her up the stairs. Her parent's bedroom door closed.

Kayla and Bradley continued to eat.

After a minute or two, Bradley said, "I can't believe you, Kayla."

Kayla looked up from her bowl. "What did I do?"

"I don't know...you just..." He shook his head.

"What?"

"It's the way you treat our parents. You need to just give them space. You're an idiot."

"No, I'm not."

"Yes, you are."

"Shut up."

"Don't tell me to shut up."

Kayla stood and walked around the table to grab Bradley's half-eaten bowl of spaghetti. "You're done."

Bradley grabbed the other end of the bowl. "No, I'm not."

They each tugged at the bowl. Bradley gave a yank and the bowl slipped from Kayla's fingers. Spaghetti and bright red sauce spewed out over the table and across the carpeted floor.

"Look what you did," Kayla said.

Bradley began to laugh. "I'm not cleaning that up."

"Yes you are. It's your fault!"

"Yeah. Right." Bradley stood, wiped a glob of sauce from his shirt. He licked his fingers and moved towards the stairs.

"Wait," Kayla said. "Clean up your mess!"

Bradley continued across the dining room. "Freak." And then he said the thing that always hurt the most: "Sometimes I really think you *were* adopted."

From down the stairs, the sounds of her parent's lovemaking came to her. It seemed louder than usual. The moaning increased to wailing, and the wailing became screaming, to her, like that of a tortured child.

TWO

She couldn't sleep. She still had that fearful feeling something significant was about to happen. In her room, by the orange glow of her desk lamp, crouched on the floor, she flipped idly through a magazine.

She eventually decided to go downstairs to get a glass of milk from the kitchen. She took the stairs slowly. She counted the steps as she descended, as she was in the habit of doing, freezing for a moment on the seventh step as it creaked—more loudly than she'd anticipated—then bounding down the final few steps, counting the floor as number fourteen.

She crept across the open darkness of the living room to the kitchen, flipped the light on, squinting against the fluorescent glow. She shivered in her pajamas. She fetched a glass from the cabinet, opened the fridge, and partially filled the glass with milk. For a moment, the air seemed to shimmer—hazy—as if a silvery veil had fallen over the world. She shook her head to clear it.

She flipped the light off. Holding her glass of milk before her, she made her way back to the stairs. The top of the stairs was dark and obscured. It was difficult to see. On the first step, the milk sloshed in the glass, running over her fingers. She gritted her teeth and continued more carefully. Which step was it that creaked? Step nine. Step ten. Had she passed it already? Twelve. Thirteen. Fourteen. Fifteen...

A voice whispered from the dark near her.

She could almost feel the weight of the empty air behind her. She glanced over her shoulder and the living room seemed far away, the shapes of the furniture gray and indistinct. Something moved about down there, she could hear it picking at things, sniffing the air in search of something. It was looking for her. It paused, turning its head toward the stairs, and Kayla caught a glimmer of eye-shine as it peered through the dark in her direction. Then it looked away. It hadn't seen her and she was relieved; she didn't want to be found.

This is an interesting dream, she thought. Why am I so scared?

When she looked back down, the creature was gone from view. She began to move up the stairs again, going up and up. Her heart was beating too quickly. The stairs concluded upon a single attic door which she'd never seen before, of heavy and roughly hewn wood, like that in an ancient castle, a large cast-iron ring in place of a doorknob. But this strange discovery didn't disturb her, the door was inviting—she was meant to go inside. It was her escape route, a safe haven from that thing lurking behind her in the dark.

Inside, it was warm—rusty hinges as the door groaned closed behind her—and a tidy little room, candles everywhere. Shelves of ancient books lined the walls of a small corridor, and then there was a small open room.

"Don't be shy. Come in," said the old woman. And she was old beyond reckoning, her face ornately wrinkled like a shriveled fruit, eyes sinking beneath her curling flesh, deep shadows—cast by the flickering candlelight—

90

drawing a mosaic of lines through her cheeks and across her lips like crosshatching on an ink drawing. In a frilly threadbare dress made for a much younger woman, she leaned back in her chair and smiled at Kayla, a smile that drew lines up either side of her face, up even to her smooth and perfectly hairless head. "It's okay. You're safe here."

And she did feel safe. She took a few steps into the room.

"Please, child. Sit down."

Kayla sunk into the only other chair in the room, setting her glass of milk down on a stack of books by the side of the chair that served as an end table. The old woman was smoking, Kayla noticed for the first time, and the white smoke was drifting and curling about the room, obscuring the her pale and wrinkled face in the cloud from her cigarette—long and thin, protruding from its quellazaire—drifting smoke like tangles of floating jellyfish. There was a book, cracked open in her lap.

"This is a dream, right?"

"I suppose," the old woman said. "Although I'm reluctant to label it as such."

Kayla felt her muscles relaxing, the tension melting from her shoulders and down over the chair beneath her.

The old woman smiled. "There is so much I wish I could show you. How things bend and move. Like liquid in the breeze. So much hurt I wish I could save you. But you're a smart girl. I'm sure you'll be alright."

Kayla looked languidly about the room. It was small, its walls circular, the floor a polished wood. All around there were books, stacked in wobbly columns like stalagmites growing from the floor. Cutouts and clippings, pictures of people and places, were anchored into the smooth mortar by crude nails—layer upon layer all over the walls. Some of these pictures, she noticed, were of naked women, like those from the magazines her father kept in a shoebox under the bed. Above the old woman there was a painting in a plain wooden frame, a beautiful landscape, a field of rolling hills and a lake, set into the wall like a window—but there were no windows; the walls were solid, climbing upwards to where the smoke obscured their further reaches.

Kayla felt a rise of excitement flow through her, even though her limbs were heavy, the chair cradling her in its warmth. This was what she'd been waiting for all day: what this woman was about to tell her...

"You might die, of course," the old woman said, her voice deep and casual. "There will be tests, and plenty of them—you can be sure of that. But I'll help you."

Kayla stared carefully into the old woman's face, to be sure she'd heard correctly, but her eyes were drawn to the slow snaking curls of smoke; she thought of fading spirits; she thought of ghosts.

"Yes. Don't worry. I will guide you, child," the old woman continued. Then she tilted her head back. "I've seen so much." She sighed. "I've walked through the Orchard of the Blood Monkeys. How I miss those days. My only concern the lilt of poetry and the wait between meals, when next I was allowed to dine on the crimson fruit. I'd spend hours discussing the philosophy of the universes with Lemmenkainen... Or we'd wonder at the existence of different animals..."

Kayla watched the old woman, unsure what she was supposed to say. The old woman took a drag on the tip of her cigarette holder, exhaled with another sigh. She seemed to fall asleep for a moment, her head nodding forward. She was so old, so very old.

"Oh, Lemm," the old woman said to the smoldering ceiling. "Remember the Looaphant? The size of a house and it could swim? And two prehensile trunks? Or was it three?"

The old woman's eyes slid closed. The cigarette holder drooped in her mouth. "I wish there was another way," she mumbled. Then a fresh cloud of smoke puffed up between Kayla and her. The old woman's liquid eyes pierced the smoke. "You have a brother, isn't that right?"

Kayla nodded.

The old woman's eyes closed again. "Good," she said. "That's good. He can help you."

Kayla tried to picture Bradley rising up next to her on a quest, standing to protect her with sword in hand, but the image was ethereal in her mind, cartoonish—laughable.

The old woman shook her head. She slumped forward.

Kayla watched the smoke swirl slowly upwards, filling the room like a tornado in time-lapse video. She tried to make out the old woman's eyes again through the haze—to gauge the old woman's intentions—but the smoke was too thick, her own eyes too bleary and unfocused. From behind the old woman's chair, another pair of eyes, with hourglass-shaped pupils, blinked once, then were gone. She heard a faint snicker.

"It's okay," the old woman said. "He's gone now, child." And Kayla knew the old woman was talking about the thing that had been looking for her in the living room. "You have so much to learn...I just hope...the fight of your life..." The old woman was asleep.

Kayla stood slowly and began to back towards the door.

"...I'll help...show you things...such things..."

Kayla pushed out of the room and down the stairway. For a moment, the stairs canted at an alarming angle and she felt her balance give way, her vision jittering dangerously. Then she was turning down the hallway and crossing to her bedroom. She had the feeling something vastly important had been shown to her, but only for a moment, and she unable to comprehend exactly what it had been.

As she struggled beneath the sheets of her bed, she thought she heard whispering, but when she remained still, there was only silence.

She felt she was being watched.

* * *

The next day—Sunday—she still had that funny feeling. As if a thundercloud loomed over her entire family, an impending storm they should be preparing for, only she was the only one aware of it—the only one to feel the charge building in the air—and no one would believe her, even if she were to try to warn them.

She thought about going outside—she needed some fresh air, some time alone to clear her head, to forget about her strange dreams from the night before—but by mid-morning, it had begun to rain and the house was filled with the low roar of the storm. She sat in her room for a while, which faced the street, watching the front-yard lawn begin to puddle, watching the trees outside swaying and dancing, the houses across the way seen as if through a gray sheet. For a moment, she thought something moved in the large cottonwood tree by the mailbox—the glint of an animal?— but it was only a branch partially broken by the storm.

Bored, and with nothing better to do, she knocked quietly on Bradley's door before stepping into her brother's room. Her brother was slouched in his beanbag chair, playing one of his games. He never took his eyes from the glowing flurry of movement on the television screen as she came up and awkwardly stood by his bed.

"How's it going, Bradley?"

"Fine. I finally beat that boss I was telling you about. Had to shoot him in the neck until his head popped off." He smiled. "The blood actually splattered the screen. It was great!"

Kayla shuffled her feet. "That's cool." She wandered over to Bradley's desk where he sometimes did schoolwork, but was mostly piled with video game boxes and booklets.

"Our parents have been bad this weekend," Bradley said. "I've just been trying to stay out of the way."

"I know what you mean," Kayla said.

"You wanna play?" Bradley asked her.

"Not really."

"Fine. Whatever." Bradley began to jab at one of the buttons on the controller with his thumb over and over. "Die! Die! Die!"

Kayla pulled the chair out from Bradley's desk and took a seat. She watched her brother play his game.

After a while, she began to aimlessly flip through the things on her brother's desk. She pushed aside a schoolbook on Pre-Algebra and brushed away several game pamphlets. She stared at Bradley's notebook and the mathematical problems he'd been working across the open page. She tried to make sense of the numbers. She'd be doing this same stuff in a couple of years. It was nonsense to her. She flipped the page...

...running through the jungle and it was chasing me and the trees had faces and they were shrieking...

...was scribbled in the margins at the top of the page in a looping line. After that: more math problems, sane and symmetrical. Kayla read the line again. She looked up at Bradley, sitting in his beanbag, killing bad guys on the screen, his face lightly flushed. She turned another page.

...my dad with a knife and a red bowtie but he wasn't my dad because he had no face...cutting myself and I couldn't stop...thick blood filling my bedroom rising and rising...something with big round eyes glowing in the darkness...trapped alone in a tiny room at the top of the stairs with no food...animals all around with accusing eyes and sharp talons scratching to get in...someone was screaming and when I woke up I realized it was me...

Kayla held her breath as she read these scribbled lines. Her wide eyes scanned the page. Her heart was a heavy warm lump inside her chest. The room had fallen silent; she was aware of nothing but her brother's notebook in front of her. She turned the page...

"What do you think you're doing?"

Kayla jumped. Bradley was standing right over her shoulder, looking down at her. His face had a glazed look, but his grin had hardened. He looked ready to commit murder. He came at her.

Kayla lurched backwards and the chair gave way with a jaunting tilt beneath her. For a moment, she felt the weightlessness of falling, then she crashed to the floor.

Bradley stepped forward, his hands reaching for her. She struggled to crawl, but her legs were twisted up in the chair. She ripped at the carpet with her nails. She could feel Bradley right behind her.

She gained her feet and ran to the door and the safety of the hallway.

"Get out of here!" Bradley screamed. He threw the closest thing at hand, the game controller.

The controller struck the wall by the door—leaving a misshapen dent in the drywall—and ricocheted in a random direction.

Kayla ran down the hallway to her room.

"Get out! Get out! Get out!"

For more information on this title and others, visit the author's website: www.KeithDeininger.com.

AFTERWARD

"Where do your ideas come from?" I am sometimes asked.

"Other worlds," I say, and smile.

I have found, as I write, as I sink into "the zone" of my work and lose myself to all else that may be happening around me, the things I produce are strange. I sit back and read over what I have written and wonder how I could have come up with such things. They seem unusual, surreal, fantastic. They seem sometimes as if they've come from someone else, or *somewhere* else. I'm a normal guy, nothing special, not that interesting to talk to. So how can a guy like me come up with such things? Where *do* they come from?

I don't have a definitive answer. But I can speculate.

There is a concept, revolving around David Lewis's ideas of *Modal Realism*, called *Fictional Realism*, which theorizes that when creative people in our world create things, they aren't really creating them so much as discovering them, that all things we consider fictitious exist in some world, on some plane of existence, somewhere in the multiverse. This would mean that creative people are those with the ability to see into other universes.

Perhaps this is what I'm doing as I write.

A little over a year ago, I became acquainted with someone who reminded me, in a lot of ways, of my younger self. His name is Colin Thorne. He shared with me the details of the summer he spent with a wealthy man in a dilapidated yet historical house. He was commissioned to paint an unusual mural in the man's basement. In the basement, when he wasn't painting, he found many old and fascinating things scattered about in boxes piled high that had clearly been undisturbed for some time, bits of history, letters and journals, clues left behind by people who had lived but are now forgotten. After some persuading on my part, he agreed to share with me a few of the things he'd found, and gave me a tattered suitcase filled with notes he'd collected.

Inside the suitcase, one of the things I found was a notebook filled with accounts of fantastic other realms, strange beasts, peoples, and cultures. It contains many stories written by a man who signs his name only as 'Marrow.' Many of the things he discusses are clearly within the realm of the fantastique, yet Marrow's writings are filled with such detail, it is difficult to imagine them to be entirely fabricated.

Shadow Animals, in its original translation, was found this way. Arranging the moldering papers until I could find some semblance of order, wiping the dust away, I discovered a story, and was immediately enthralled. It was written in an entirely different style from what I have written above, of course, in a language that does not yet belong to any cultural group in existence in this world, but I hope I have done it justice. I can only urge readers to be understanding and cognizant of the translation and interpretation I have provided.

And this is only the beginning. Much of Marrow's accounts take place in a world he calls Meridian. It is a world vastly different from our own in many ways, yet similar in others, and they are inexplicably linked. It is Meridian, I believe, where Saul and Ezzy find themselves in *Shadow Animals*.

My plan is to produce more stories set in this world—in translation, of course. Collected, these stories—linked by a common mythology, if not by narrative—will comprise the Meridian Codex. *Shadow Animals* is a Meridian Codex story, as is *Marrow's Pit*. Expect others to follow, including a larger novel, as I am hard at work.

Keith Deininger
June 20th, 2014

ABOUT THE AUTHOR

An award-winning writer and poet, Keith Deininger is the author of *The New Flesh, Fevered Hills, Marrow's Pit, Shadow Animals, Ghosts of Eden, The Hallow* and *Within*. He was raised in the American Southwest and currently resides in Albuquerque, New Mexico with his wife and their four dogs. He is a skeptic.

For more, visit www.KeithDeininger.com.

Also, consider joining his New Release Mailing List (keithdeininger.com/new-release-mailing-list) for a free story, the occasional bonus material, and to be the first to hear when he has a new release.

24002265R00061

Printed in Great Britain
by Amazon